for the Love of the Viscount

The Noble Hearts, Book 1

CALLIE HUTTON

This book is a work of fiction. Names, characters, places, and incidents are the product of the author's imagination or are used fictitiously. Any resemblance to actual events, locales, or persons, living or dead, is coincidental.

Author's website: http://calliehutton.com/
Cover design by Erin Dameron-Hill
Manufactured in the United States of America

First Edition March 2017

ISBN-10: 154497972X
ISBN-13: 978-1544979724

ABOUT THE BOOK

Bluestocking Lady Elise Smith is a very content spinster. She holds intellectual gatherings and attends poetry readings, mind-improving lectures, and art shows. She runs her father's household with quiet and determined efficiency, which is why she is absolutely stunned when Papa informs his three daughters that until Lady Elise is happily settled with—gasp—a husband, he will not consider offers for his two younger daughters.

Lord Simon St. George has happily watched one friend after another become leg-shackled, taking pride in the fact that his title is secured by a brother and nephew, so there is no reason to seek a wife for himself. When he sees a woman previously unknown to him at a ball, who seems to be hiding from the rest of the attendees, he is intrigued enough to introduce himself.

Simon sees a lovely, intelligent woman to pass the time with. Elise sees a man who can help her thwart her father by pretending they are courting. But even the best plans can go awry…

DEDICATION

To all the amazing vocalists whose music I listened to while writing *For the Love of the Viscount.* Thanks for the inspiration.

ACKNOWLEDGMENTS AND AUTHOR'S NOTES

The wonderful members of The Beau Monde offer so much in the way of guidance and information to keep all of us Regency authors on track. Thank you all so much for your help.

My family keeps me anchored. When the pressure is too much and the words simply won't come, they are always good for a laugh.

The folk tale collection entitled Grimms' Fairy Tales, containing the story of Cinderella, was published in 1812.

Elise was a well-read woman, and smart. Simon did substitute the name Elise for Delia when he read *Tell me, My Heart if This Be Love* by George Lyttelton, 1st Baron Lyttelton

PROLOGUE

London, England
March, 1818

The Right Honorable, the Earl of Pomeroy, sat at the head of his dinner table and smiled at his three lovely daughters, who smiled back at him. Three *unmarried* lovely daughters. Each one was charming and pretty in her own way. And each one needed to find a husband and remove herself from his benevolence before he went broke.

The bills continued to pile up on the desk in his study. Bonnets, gowns, gloves, slippers, ribbons. The list was endless. While he had no doubt his two youngest daughters, Lady Juliet and Lady Marigold, would one day find their way to the altar, he had no expectations that his eldest, Lady Elise at three and twenty, would ever wander in that direction. Without a little push, that was.

Which he was about to give.

"My dears, I would like your attention, if you please." He smiled at the loves of his life. Obedient as ever, they all gave him their utmost attention. One pair of blue eyes, two hazel.

"Yes, Papa?" Elise, one of the pair of hazel eyes, said.

He cleared this throat. "It has come to my attention that perhaps I have been remiss in assuring all of you secure the best in life. Everything that your blessed mother—" he made the sign of the cross "—and I, had together. Love, marriage, children."

Julie and Marigold continued to smile, but Elise stiffened and a frown marred her comely face. *Ah, yes.* That was expected.

"Of course we wish that for ourselves as well," his youngest darling, Lady Marigold, said. A true treasure, and the image of her exquisite mother.

"Indeed."

"Papa, I believe we spoke of this before." Elise patted her mouth with her serviette and laid it alongside her plate. "Marigold and Juliet are well suited to marriage, but I thought we agreed I would continue on here with you. You know I do an excellent job of managing your house."

"And my life as well, my dear." He gave her a well-rehearsed fatherly smile.

"What did you have in mind, Papa? The Season is just starting, and I hope to find my true love this year." Juliet, at nine and ten years, brought sunshine and happiness to his life. Along with a pile of bills for jewelry and shoes. Lord, the girl loved shoes and dance slippers. She must dance every dance at every ball since she went through two pairs at each event.

"I believe the best way to assure each of you has what every woman dreams of is a sensible method I have spent many a night deciding on."

Two of his daughters stared at him with excitement since it sounded as though this was a plan to help them obtain their wishes and hopes. Alas, Elise apparently found the conversation disturbing. She did not look in his eyes when he gazed at her. He was aware his normal look of adoration had a bit of determination in it.

"What have you decided, Papa? Since I have no interest in marriage—*as you well know*—this plan is most likely for my sisters. I want to be sure it will be the best idea for them." She wagged her finger at him. "You do come up with a scheme that is less than ideal on occasion, in which case I have needed to direct you toward another avenue."

Yes the love of my heart, you spend a great deal of time directing.

The moment had arrived. "It seems fair to me that you should all find your husbands in order." He sat back and beamed as if he'd discovered the secret of longevity.

His beloved Elise frowned. "In order of what?"

"Birth."

Elise continued to stare at him, her mouth agape.

Juliet asked, "Birth?"

"Yes, my dear hearts. We will spend the next weeks seeing that our darling Elise finds her perfect match, as she is the firstborn of my delightful progeny."

Juliet and Marigold gasped in horror and looked at their sister. Elise had made it known quite loudly, and often, that she had no intention of marrying. Ever.

Elise cleared her through. "Papa, I assume you are joking with us."

He turned his attention to her, forcing his steely determination to overwhelm the adoration. "No, my precious. It came to me in a dream where I saw your beloved mother who took me to task for allowing you to flounder when I should be guiding you."

"Flounder? Guiding?" His poor girl's face was pale, her breathing rapid.

She seemed to steady herself and put forth her brightest smile. "Oh, Papa. While I appreciate your concern for my future, I believe we can turn our efforts and attention to Juliet." Her lips tightened, and she glared at her sister, apparently looking for support.

"I agree, Papa. I would love to have help from all of you in securing my future." His sweet second eldest nudged Marigold with her elbow.

"Ouch. Yes, Papa, I think Juliet is definitely the one we should be focused on. My turn will be next year." Marigold rubbed her side and cast a reproving glance at her sister.

"Oh, my enchanting offspring, how I love you so. However, my mind is made up. We will see Elise a happy bride this year." He beamed at them, looking from one cherished daughter to the next. 'Twas time for others—with hefty bank rolls—to cherish them as well.

"Papa, suppose I refuse?" Elise had never gone against his wishes in her entire life. She had always been able to persuade him to see things her way. Which was another advantage to his plan. She would be directing someone else's life.

"Then, my dear, I am afraid it will take longer for your sisters to find their own true loves. You see, I will be unable to accept suitors for them until you are safely settled in your own little love nest." With that pronouncement he stood and gave them a slight bow. "Now if you will excuse me, I will retire to my library and enjoy a brandy before bed."

Three girls sat opened-mouth as he smiled at them and left the room. He strode down the corridor, lighthearted. He'd put his plan into action, and soon he would be free of bills. Not that he begrudged his treasured daughters their fribbles, but a man could not watch his fortune dwindle every day without concern.

Although he had no son to whom he would pass along his title and money, it still disturbed him to watch his balance shrink monthly.

Grinning to himself, he poured a brandy and sat by the fireplace, raising a toast to freedom.

CHAPTER ONE

Elise stood in front of the full length mirror in her bedchamber and stared at herself. The deep green silk gown with gold trim looked stunning on her. Charlene, the lady's maid she shared with her sisters, had managed to fix her usual unruly hair and arranged it in some sort of topknot type thing.

Long white satin gloves covered her hands and arms, and lovely green satin slippers peeked out from under the hem of her gown. Her mother's pearls surrounded her throat, with the matching earbobs dangling from her ears.

She felt utterly ridiculous.

This woman in the mirror was not Lady Elise Smith, accepted bluestocking, sworn spinster, and hostess of well-respected gatherings of the intellectual elite of London. This woman was on the prowl for a husband. Something she never, ever wanted.

She still could not believe she couldn't persuade Papa to dispense with this crazy idea. She'd laughed, cajoled, teased, and even—God help her—stamped her foot like a child. He was adamant.

Her, married! Married women had no freedom. They did what their husbands decided they should do. They bore children and held balls and soirees. They made morning calls where they shared the latest gossip.

Never did any married woman she know browse the shelves of Hatchard's bookstore in anticipation of a lively debate later that evening with knowledgeable friends.

And to hold her sisters' happiness as a threat if she did not consent to this ridiculousness was the absolute worst thing Papa could have done.

Elise had been mother and sister to Marigold and Juliet from the time they were five and six years, when their mother had died from consumption. She'd taken over the mother role, and by four and ten years, the well-being of her father, also. It was she who kept track of his social calendar, who met with Cook and the housekeeper to make certain his home ran smoothly, and assured his cigars were always available and his brandy at his fingertips.

And now he was throwing her to the lions. *Not well done, Papa.*

"Elise, you look fabulous." Juliet burst into her room with Marigold following, both of them full of excitement and happiness. Charlene had apparently finished with them, also, since they were both dressed in beautiful gowns with becoming hairstyles.

"I look ludicrous." She turned from the mirror and faced her sisters. "And I feel silly." She pinched the sides of her gown and held her hands out. "This is not me."

Marigold sat on her bed. "I know, but you do look wonderful."

Elsie reached for her fan, shawl, and reticule. "What I am hoping is I will attend a few of these affairs and after receiving no attention—which I am counting on, by the way—Papa will understand this whole idea of me marrying is as foolish as I look."

Marigold and Juliet looked at each other.

"What?"

"I really don't think with the way you look that you won't receive any attention," Juliet said. "Also, you are what the *ton* calls new blood. You have not appeared in a ballroom in a few years."

"Smartly so, I might add." Elise walked to the door and opened it. "We might as well move along. This disaster of an evening will not commence until I get there to make it happen."

"Papa!" Elise stopped at the bottom of the stairs and regarded her father. He had not attended a *ton* ball, as far as Elise knew, for several years. Yet here he stood in formal clothes, looking very handsome, she might add, ready to escort his daughters to the Cummings' ball.

"Papa, you look splendid." Juliet walked up to him and kissed him on the cheek. "You are such a fine escort for us."

"I asked my cousin, Florence, to again act as chaperone for the Season, but she was unable to take up those duties, so I am afraid you are stuck with me and whoever else I might coerce into the role." He looked at Elise. "My dearest Elise, you are a vision of loveliness."

It was hard to remain angry with Papa. He was such a sweet man and merely wanted what was best for his daughters. The only way she could persuade him away from this benighted plan was to not encourage any men and spend her time as close to a potted plant as she could. Once he realized the likelihood of her attracting men was hopeless, he would abandon his scheme and all would return to normal.

In a flurry of gowns, laughter, and teasing, the family descended the stairs and entered the Pomeroy carriage. Elise stared out the window, annoyed at herself for the feeling of anxiety churning in her stomach. She had no reason to be nervous. The people who attended these functions, and their opinions, meant nothing to her. Of course she wouldn't measure up. She was Lady Eloise, the bluestocking, most likely the joke of polite society.

That was fine with her. She had her purpose in life, and it did not encompass being a flighty debutante in search of a husband. She was respected and well thought of. In her circle of friends, of course. Those who believed flaunting oneself dressed like a peacock for the sole purpose of dragging some poor bloke to the altar was derisory.

The carriage drew up to the front door of the Cummings' townhouse, and Elise's dinner seemed to want to make a reappearance. She tamped down her foolishness. She was an earl's daughter. A person in her own right, with friends, and held in high regard.

Papa stepped out and turned to assist his daughters. He did look wonderful tonight. He was still a handsome man, a devoted father, and in some cases—like now—a stubborn, unreasonable man.

He tucked her arm into his, and, with Juliet and Marigold following behind them, he led them up the path and to the door where the butler took their invitation. They joined the queue of guests as they were announced. Once their names were called, they descended the steps. Elise felt as though she were going to faint.

There were so many people! And they were all

staring at the four of them. Her mouth dried up, and she gripped Papa's arm so tightly, it would be a wonder if he didn't have bruises in the morning.

He patted her hand "Relax, daughter. 'Tis only a ball." He led them through the throng, stopping on occasion to talk with a friend, and each time introduced Elise, who was mostly unknown to the Quality crowd. Several women stepped into his path and bantered with him, which startled Elise. He wrote his name on a few dance cards, which stunned her further.

Marigold and Juliet had left them as soon as they reached the ballroom to visit with their friends. Elise, of course, had no friends here. Her friends were busy with important things, not dressing up in silly clothes and bowing and curtseying left and right.

"I am placing you and your sisters into the hands of Lady Dearborn for the evening, my dear. She will act as chaperone, since I will be visiting the card room in between the dances I have promised." Papa presented her to an older lady who stood with other matrons and regarded Elise through her quizzing glass. From the expression on her face, she did not seem to find her wanting. She hated that the woman's apparent approval relieved her.

"Go on to the card room, my lord. I will be happy to watch over the young ladies." Lady Dearborn actually cast him a saucy look, and Elise almost made the *faux pas* of snorting. To think women wanted to flirt with Papa!

Then she gave him a second glance and saw what perhaps a lot of women had seen since they'd arrived. Tall, handsome, light brown hair with a bit of silver, piercing blue eyes, and a genuine smile. She shook her head. Here she was at her first ball since her come-out season and she was having ludicrous thoughts. That was what polite society did to one's brain.

"My dear, why is it I have never met you before?" Once again the quizzing glass rose to Lady Dearborn's eye.

"I have not moved about in Society for a few years, my lady."

"Indeed? And why is that? Have you been unwell?"

Good lord, was she going to be questioned on end by the woman? How would she escape this interrogation without giving offense?

"No. I just prefer other types of pursuits." When the older woman continued to stare at her, she added, "I enjoy reading, the museums and art galleries, small gatherings, and poetry readings."

Lady Dearborn's eyes grew wide. "A bluestocking?"

Elise raised her chin. "Yes, my lady. I am afraid that is what I am."

To Elise's surprise, the woman actually chuckled. "And your father intends to marry you off?"

Elise winced at the forthright question. "I am afraid that is his plan."

"I sense you are not in agreement with his plan." Lady Dearborn's eyes shifted and she looked over Elise's shoulder. "Ah, good evening, St. George."

A young man stepped into view. He was tall, almost a foot over Elise's five feet four inches. His reddish brown hair brushed his forehead and teased the edge of his cravat at the back of his neck. Although he directed his question to Lady Dearborn, his deep blue eyes regarded Elise. "May I have the pleasure of an introduction, Lady Dearborn?"

"Of course, my dear. Lady Elise Smith, eldest daughter of Lord Pomeroy, may I present to you, Lord Simon, Viscount St. George."

Elise curtsied and St. George bowed. "May I add my name to your dance card, my lady?"

Flustered at being asked to dance so soon when she was fully expecting to hide behind furniture all evening, she fumbled until St. George caught the card dangling from her wrist and quickly added his name. By this time she was flushed and remembered precisely why she hated these events. She always felt out of place.

***

Simon tried not to grin at Lady Elise's obvious agitation. He'd never seen her before and was curious, since she was apparently several years out of the schoolroom. Beautiful was a fitting word, although her face also showed strength and intelligence. Her chestnut brown hair had been drawn back, with curls already escaping the intricate style.

Warm hazel eyes revealed poorly hidden annoyance. This was a woman who was not in her usual environment and she did not like it. Curiosity turned to intrigue. Although Simon had no interest in marriageable ladies, since he had no intention of ever marrying himself, something about this woman called to him to know more.

Giving her time to compose herself, Simon turned to Lady Dearborn. "My lady, you are looking splendid, as usual."

"Don't turn your charm on me, dear boy. Save it for the young ladies." Her slight blush belied her words. Simon had found ladies liked compliments, no matter how old they were. It was a trait that made him quite popular with the female set.

"Are you new to London, Lady Elise? I am acquainted with your sisters." Now that she had stopped fussing with the dance card, he turned his attention to her.

"Not new to London, but certainly new to these types of events." She waved her hand around, smacking Lord Nettleson, who stood behind her, in the arm with her fan. "Oh, please forgive me, my lord."

The man had walked up behind her, most likely looking for an introduction, as well. Nettleson bowed. "No forgiveness needed, my lady." He bowed to Lady Dearborn. "May I beg an introduction to your lovely companion?"

And so it began. Before the orchestra played its first note, Lady Elise had several names written on her dance card. Simon refused to relinquish his spot next to her, though, as the men came and went. A few lingered, but he saw no reason to move on since his was the first dance of the evening. Which he hoped was a waltz.

As luck would have it, the first dance was a country reel, hardly giving him the opportunity to discover why Lady Elise did not usually attend these events and how she came to be here tonight.

It was a question he asked of himself many times. Since balls, assemblies, routs, and the like were known to be the hunting ground for husbands, one would think he would stay far away. But he actually enjoyed these affairs. Dodging marriage-minded mamas had become a game with him. But rarely did he meet a woman who actually made him want to know her.

Not just to dance and banter with, but learn about her, the woman.

Good grief, next he would be spouting philosophy, or worse yet, writing bad poetry. He extended his hand. "My lady, I believe this is our dance."

She took his hand, but instead of tucking it under his arm, she continued to cling to it. They joined the line of dancers and faced each other. Before the music began, she leaned toward him and whispered, "It has been quite some time since I danced, my lord. I am terribly afraid I will make a muck of it."

The steps of country reels could be quite intricate, so he understood her anxiety. "'Tis amazing how these things come back to you when needed. However I will help you, so no worries."

Seldom had he been so wrong about something. The music began, and after only a few minutes, it was quite obvious not only was Lady Elise making a muck of it, she was confusing those next to them on either side. Curious glances in their direction turned to tightened lips and *sotto voice* comments as the dance continued, and Lady Elise stumbled her way through it.

After several more minutes of watching his partner suffer, he took matters into his own hands. Once again they came together and joined hands, but instead of walking in a circle, he tugged her away from the line and practically dragged her toward the French doors. She giggled as they wove their way through the crowd. Not the silly, high-pitched giggle of the young debutants, but a rich, deep sound that went straight to his cock.

Once they were outside, she leaned against the

balustrade and, clutching her middle, released a full-throated laugh. Unable to resist, he joined her until they were both wiping tears from their eyes.

"That was terrible," she gulped, still trying to catch her breath.

Who was this woman with the ability to laugh at herself? There wasn't one debutante he could think of who would not have collapsed into a fit of tears and hysteria if that had happened to her on the dance floor. "You were quite serious when you said it had been a while since you danced."

"Yes. Indeed." She stood upright and pushed away from the balustrade. "I apologize for embarrassing you, my lord."

"No apology needed. You have given me the best laugh of the month—perhaps the year." He extended his arm. "How about a stroll in the garden?"

"Yes. I think I can manage that since I've been walking for a number of years now." She took his arm and they made their way down the steps and into the gas-lit garden. She inhaled deeply. "I love the smell of flowers after rain."

"And we have had enough of that lately." Hell, he did not want to discuss the weather with this unique woman. "Why is it you have not been in Society for some time?" He imagined family deaths and illnesses.

"Polite society would be shocked, and I should probably not tell you this, but I am a bluestocking." She lowered her voice and glanced from side to side, even though there was no one else about.

He found her delightful and himself enchanted.

"Through and through. A committed spinster and a lover of books, intellectual gatherings, and the museums." She smiled. "There you have it. Lady Elise Smith with all her foils and foibles."

He stopped and turned her toward him. Reaching out, he tucked a curl behind her ear. "Not foils and foibles to my way of thinking." Before he could do something stupid, since they'd only just met, he resumed their walk. "So why is it you are here tonight? Is it not the social whirl where ladies attempt to snare husbands?"

She let out a deep sigh. "Papa."

"What?"

Lady Elise moved them toward a stone bench under an oak tree. He sat alongside her, feeling the warmth of her body next to him, but missing the contact of her arm nestled in his. "Papa has always allowed me my freedom and never questioned my decision to not marry. For some ungodly reason, he decided quite recently that unless I marry, he would not consider offers from gentlemen for my two younger sisters."

His brows rose. "Not well done of him, I'm afraid."

"Indeed. You see, our mother passed away when I was ten years and my sisters were six and five. I've been the only mother they've known since them. Papa knew the best way to have me agree to his plan was to threaten my sisters' happiness." She shook her head, the curls at her temples dancing. "So I agreed to attend social functions with the intention of finding a husband."

He grinned. "A change of heart?"

"No." Her eyes grew wide and she drew back, looking as though he'd asked her to dance another country reel. "Not at all. I do not want a husband.

Ever. From what I've seen, they direct their wives' lives, still maintain their own freedom, and a woman must bear it all with a smile."

"So I take it your plan is to confuse and cripple every dance partner you have so no one will offer for you?" He grinned, unable to help how easy it was to do so in her company.

She tapped her finger on her chin, pretending to consider it. "That would be a good idea, but no." She glanced sideways at him, a devilish smile on her lovely face. "What I have decided is to avoid notice by spending time at balls hiding behind potted plants and taking a number of breaks in the ladies' retiring room."

"No. It won't work."

She eyed him with raised eyebrows. "Why not?"

He touched her cheek. So soft. "You are too beautiful to hide behind anything."

Lady Elise stilled, and then a slight blush rose from her neckline to her hairline. Had no one ever told her of her arresting appeal? Did she not have a mirror in her bedchamber? No woman who looked like her could avoid men. In fact, were she to dress in ashes and sackcloth, he doubted she would go unnoticed.

"Thank you for your kind words, my lord. But that is still my plan." She shrugged. "I have no other."

"Please call me Simon. 'Tis my given name and my friends use it." He took her hand in his. "I hope we can be friends."

Her eyes narrowed. "Only friends."

Friends it would have to be. Although he'd felt a pull toward Lady Elise from the time he'd first laid eyes on her, he also was not interested in marriage. If not the wedded state, one did not have any other type of relationship with a gently reared woman, except friendship. "Yes. Agreed. You see I have been dodging the marriage-minded mamas of the *ton* for a few years myself. I know how to hold their darling daughters at arm's length. I could give you some tips and be your cohort in crime, as it were."

"Why would you do that?"

"Because I love a challenge," he gave her a wink, "and keeping away the hordes of men who will descend upon you is a true test of my abilities."

CHAPTER TWO

Elise drew on her gloves and made her way downstairs. Last night's event had turned out quite well. She had been forced to accept more dances with gentlemen who had requested them and found after the first few she'd remembered most of the steps. She did stumble on occasion but felt she had acquitted herself nicely.

Otherwise, Simon had kept her occupied with walks in the garden and a waltz. Which had disturbed her more than she would have liked. Although she knew the steps of that dance, she'd never engaged in it with another person besides her sisters or their dance master, who was old and pudgy.

When Simon had drawn her into his arms, she immediately felt odd, nothing like herself. His warm hand on her lower back, as he moved her around the floor, seemed to burn right through to her skin. For as lively and chatty she had been with him up until then, she found herself unable to do more than stare at him.

At one point as their eyes locked, something flickered in his expression that had her wishing they could take another cooling stroll in the garden. Her stomach did strange things, and she felt the need to press closer to him. During a turn he did pull her nearer and she almost lost her breath. He'd grinned.

Once the dance had ended, he escorted her back to Lady Dearborn but stayed by her side. A few more men came and went, but Simon never budged. He was funny and enjoyed pointing out the ridiculous to her. A woman's turban with a stuffed bird nesting on it, Lord Mathison's cane with the head of a lion at the top, Lord Walton who still clung to his much out-of-date wig. When they were speaking with others, he would lean in and whisper something about them that had her biting her lip to keep from laughing out loud.

The man was outrageous.

Once Simon left, mentioning a meeting at his club, she'd sent a message to Papa that she was suffering from a megrim, and requested he send for the carriage to return her home. It seemed once her cohort had left, the fun at the ball had left with him. She arrived home hours before her sisters.

Simon had suggested a ride in Hyde Park today. He said if other men thought he had a claim on her, some of them would back off. She certainly hoped so. She'd been dismayed to find four large bouquets of flowers with her name on them when she'd arrived for breakfast. Papa beamed, and she felt the muscles in her stomach tighten.

Simon's plan had better work.

If she could get through the Season with no one approaching Papa with an offer, she might convince him she was truly unmarriageable. He would stop this nonsense and allow her sisters to find husbands. But for now she would enjoy a ride in the park with someone by whom she did not need to feel threatened. Simon had absolutely no interest in marriage, so they were perfectly partnered.

The day was warm and lovely, perfect for a ride. Simon, standing at the entrance hall waiting on her, dressed in tan breeches, Hessian boots, a dark blue jacket, and starched cravat, did strange things to parts of her body to which she normally only gave a passing thought. She shook her head. That was silly. This was Simon, her cohort in crime. The man scaring off other men so she could go through the Season without anyone troubling her with an offer of marriage.

He had arrived in a lovely gig, just large enough for the two of them. Since she was past the age of needing constant supervision, this sort of vehicle was fine, especially since it was open. Elise unfurled her parasol and rested it on her shoulder and spun it around, grinning. She had always eschewed any type of courting but found it could be quite pleasant riding along the park path with a handsome man at her side.

However, it was important to keep reminding herself that nothing was more important than her independence. Years of taking care of her family, making decisions, and following her own path for happiness was ingrained in her. She wanted a life of freedom and intellectual pursuits. She would leave the bending to a husband's wishes, and producing an heir and a spare, to her sisters and instead take on the role of the doting aunt.

But there was no reason whatsoever that she could not enjoy the attention she was receiving from St. George. Courting with no expectations. Perfect.

"You look like the cat that stole the cream." He grinned at her, his reddish brown curls blowing against his forehead in the soft breeze.

"Do I now?" She smiled and dipped her head,

realizing she was practically flirting. Good lord, would she be batting her eyelashes next? She had to rein herself in and remind her fluttering heart this was all pretend. Which was precisely what she wanted.

"I was just thinking how pleasant it could be having a gentleman's company and not having to worry about him eyeing me up to be his brood mare."

Simon burst out laughing, causing a few heads to turn in their direction. "Elise, you have a way with words, I must say that."

"Well, 'tis true. Most men would never allow themselves to be leg-shackled if they didn't feel the responsibility to their title." She studied him. "By the way, why is it you are so against marriage? Don't you have a title to secure?"

"No. I have a title, of course, Viscount St. George, but my younger brother has a son. He is only two years old—my nephew, not my brother—so that that gives me two males to inherit should I leave this earth prematurely."

Although he jested, a sudden wave of sadness washed over her at the idea of Simon no longer around to tease her, be her partner, and suffer though other dances with her. She pushed that melancholy thought away as nonsense. After all, they'd only just met, and she barely knew the man.

"That is interesting. I eschew marriage because I don't want to lose my freedom and bow to a man's wishes. Since men have all the power and control, why are you satisfied in having your brother and nephew inherit?"

He shrugged, but Elise got a glimpse of his eyes before he turned his head, where she saw pain. Something had happened to put him off marriage.

"No particular reason. Maybe I prefer to not answer to a wife."

Accepting his answer was probably the wisest thing to do. Instead of further questioning, she nodded to three ladies who were riding in a landau alongside them. One of the women waved her hand. "Oh, Lord St. George, I hoped to speak with you. Can you pull over?"

"That would be a bit difficult, Lady Townsend. Perhaps I can call at your home?"

"Yes, wonderful, my lord. I will expect you tomorrow. My calling hours are from three to five." She gave another wave and her driver pulled ahead of them.

Simon ran his finger around the inside of his cravat. "Will you be available tomorrow at three o'clock?"

Elise gave him a half-smile. "Yes, I can be. By any chance will you be escorting me to Lady Townsend's home?"

He snapped the reins. "I knew from the very first that you were a very bright woman, Elise."

***

Simon saw Elise up the steps to her townhome and hurried back down to his gig. It had been quite some time since he'd enjoyed himself so much with a young lady. This young lady had no expectations of marriage offers or plans to conspire to have them caught in a compromising situation to force his hand. He could enjoy her company without worry.

And enjoy her company, he did. Elise was certainly easy to look at and fun at the same time. He could tease her without shocked indrawn breaths, blushing faces, or tears. It was a rare woman who could laugh at herself. He smiled as he drove away, actually looking forward to calling on Lady Townsend the next afternoon.

As long as he had Elise by his side to avoid Lady Townsend's desperate-for-a-husband daughter, Miss Abbott. He knew that had been behind Lady Townsend wanting to speak with him, hence the afternoon call. She'd been trying for over a year to push the two of them together. Even if he'd been in the market for a wife—thank you, no—Miss Abbott would never be his choice.

Pretty and petulant, she would make a man's life flat out miserable. He whistled as he continued on his way home, not having felt this cheerful in a long time.

***

The next afternoon he pulled up in front of the Pomeroy townhouse and was admitted by their butler. He no sooner requested Lady Elise than Lord Pomeroy came barreling down the corridor. "Lord St. George, just the man I wanted to see." He held out his hand which Simon took, a bit uneasy at the man's enthusiastic greeting.

Pomeroy slapped him on the back. "Come on down to my study, boy. Let's have something a bit stronger than what you're going to get at Townsend's place."

Apparently the man knew he was escorting Elise this afternoon and most likely that he'd taken her on a ride the prior afternoon. He shoved away the uneasy feeling since this had been their plan. He would pretend to have an interest in her to keep away any serious suitors. Then when the Season was over, he would wish her well, go on his merry way, and she would be off the hook with looking for a husband.

So why did he feel as though he was being scrutinized as a potential son-in-law? A position he no intention of ever seeking.

Pomeroy pointed to a chair. "It will be a while before my daughter makes an appearance; you know how the ladies are." He grinned and almost bounced over to the sideboard. Simon could easily see where Elise got her good nature. Pomeroy poured two glasses of brandy and handed one to Simon, settling in the chair across from him.

"Daughters are a wonderful thing." Pomeroy took a sip of brandy. "Wouldn't trade any one of them for the world." He looked off into the distance and took another sip, then leaned forward as if offering a secret. "But they are deuced expensive, my boy. Damned deuced expensive." He shook his head and took another sip.

He mused for a minute or two, then pointed his finger. "One day you will find out. I always thought boys would be flattening my pockets, what with University, drinking, gambling, mistresses, that sort of thing." He studied his empty glass as if confused why there wasn't any liquor left.

Putting the glass aside, he said, "St. George. A viscount, correct?"

"Yes, sir."

Pomeroy nodded as if pleased. "Elise has a nice dowry, you know. Very nice. Cheaper than keeping her in gowns and folderols for a lifetime, though."

Simon was in the process of taking a drink when that statement came out of his host's mouth. He coughed, barely able to keep from spewing the liquor all over himself. Rather than dismissing the man's remarks, he had to pretend interest if they were to fool everyone about their attachment.

"Good to hear, my lord." Bloody hell, where was Elise? If she took much longer, he feared Pomeroy would lock the study door and whip out a marriage contract.

"There you are." Elise entered the room and Simon almost choked once again. She wore a white and yellow striped afternoon gown. Her hair was pulled back in some type of a top knot, with a yellow ribbon tied around her hair. A yellow and white bonnet swung from her fingers.

The neckline of the gown was low enough to make his mouth water. She brought sunshine into the room with her. Not just with her outfit, but with the bright smile that did strange things to his insides. He felt like an idiot when Pomeroy coughed as Simon just kept staring at her. He jumped up, forgetting he held a glass of liquid. It crashed to the floor, but luckily none of the liquid splashed on him.

Elise giggled that deep laugh that drove him crazy, as it had the night before. It would be best if they removed themselves before he made a complete cake of himself in front of her father. He turned to the man. "If you will excuse us, my lord."

Humor in his eyes, Pomeroy waved him off. "Have a good time."

Simon helped Elise into the gig and they were on their way. The day was perfect, and the nice weather had him thinking about taking her on a picnic sometime soon. He could have his cook fix a basket of his favorite things. There was a perfect spot just outside of London where they could spend the afternoon, eating and chatting away.

Since he'd learned of her interests, there were

several books he wanted to share with her. Maybe an afternoon at the art gallery would be pleasant, as well.

Then he brought himself up short.

What the devil was he thinking? This was no real courtship. He only had to hold other men at bay until the end of the Season, which was only necessary at pubic outings. Based on the flowers he'd seen in the drawing room as Lord Pomeroy had escorted him down the corridor, he hadn't done a decent job of it the night before. Hopefully, a few were for her sisters.

He hoped bringing Elise with him to Lady Townsend's might help *him* with her machinations. He would help Elise, and she, in turn, would help him. This could be a very productive association. Yes, that's what it was. An association, nothing more.

The room was already filled with three young ladies and two gentlemen when they arrived. Lady Townsend was too well mannered to show disdain that he'd brought Elise with him, but unfortunately her daughter was not.

Miss Abbott narrowed her eyes at Elise and then greeted him with a bright smile. "It was so nice of you to come, Lord St. George." She nudged the woman alongside her, almost shoving her off the settee. The poor flustered guest rose and moved to another chair. "Please sit here, my lord. It will be so much easier to converse."

***

Elise did a fine job of holding her grin at Miss Abbott's maneuver. She sat on a deep green and white striped armless settee next to a gentleman she did not know. But then, with the scant time she'd spent in polite society, there were very few men she did know.

He placed the teacup balanced on his knee onto the small table in front of him. "May I introduce myself?" He stood and bowed. "The Earl of Warwick at your service."

Elise offered her hand. "How do you do, my lord. I am Lady Elise Smith, daughter of Lord Pomeroy."

He regained his seat and leaned a little too close. "I can't believe I've never met you before now."

She leaned back. "I don't go about in society much."

He offered her a seductive smile. "Ah, yes. Apparently not. You, I would never forget. I know your sisters, lovely girls, but they never mentioned they were hiding the most beautiful one at home." He gazed into her eyes, with what she was sure he thought a seductive look, but it only made her giggle.

The sound of someone clearing his throat caught Elise and Warwick's attention. Simon sat glaring at Elise, ignoring Miss Abbott who chattered on and on. Whatever was wrong? He looked ready to throttle someone. She turned to look over her shoulder, but there was no one behind her who would warrant that sort of glare.

A footman stood in front of her, holding out a tray with cups of tea and small plates of pastries. "My lady?"

Grateful to have a way to distract her from Lord Warwick's attention, she accepted a cup, glancing once again at Simon to see him still glaring at her. She raised her eyebrows in question, and he nodded in Warwick's direction. Before she could decipher what he was trying to say to her, Warwick turned his back to the group and moved in closer, virtually sealing them off from Simon and the rest of the room.

"Why have you not given us the pleasure of your company before now, Lady Elise?"

"I prefer other activities." She took a sip of her tea, reminding herself why she did not venture into Society much. The man was getting on her nerves, and she had the urge to dump the cup of tea into his lap.

"Such as?" He studied her with an intensity that disturbed her. She'd always seen humor and teasing in Simon's eyes. Not so in this man. This man made her decidedly uncomfortable.

It took her a moment to remember what they were talking about. She moved back slightly but felt herself slipping off the settee, so she stayed where she was. "I enjoy poetry readings and intellectual gatherings."

"Ah, a bluestocking." He grinned and somehow she felt as though he was laughing at her. She decided at that moment that she didn't like Lord Warwick very much. He reached out and took her hand. "Perhaps I may attend one of your intellectual gatherings." She tried to tug her hand back, but he was not allowing her to do that.

Even though she rarely ventured out on morning calls, she knew his behavior was inappropriate. Her only recourse was to dump the tea in his lap.

"Lady Elise." At the sound of her name, she looked past Warwick, pulling her hand free with just enough force that she jerked backward. With arms flailing, she slid off the settee, landing on her bottom, her skirts sliding up to her knees. The teacup in her hand flew into the air, splashing the liquid on both her and Warwick.

A hush fell over the room, so her "Ouch" was clearly heard by all. Before Warwick could even reach down for her, Simon was by her side, pushing down her gown and pulling her to her feet.

He held her around the waist and turned toward Lady Townsend and Miss Abbott. "I am so sorry, ladies, but I feel I must escort Lady Elise home. She seems to have hurt herself."

Elise didn't know whether to elbow Simon in the middle or stomp on Warwick's foot. Before she could do either or say a word, he had whisked her out of the room. "My carriage, please."

"Lord St. George." Miss Abbott hurried from the room. "I meant to give you this." She handed him a cream-colored envelope.

He bowed. "Thank you, Miss Abbott. I bid you a pleasant afternoon." He took Elise's arm and they left the house. The carriage was just pulling up when they descended the steps.

Once they settled in, Simon snapped the reins. "What was Warwick about?" He stared straight ahead, his lips tight.

Elise drew herself up. "Just one minute. I did not hurt myself, as you blurted out to one and all, and furthermore, I did not need for you to race across the room and rescue me."

Ignoring her indignation, he continued, "From what I saw, Warwick was out of line."

"Perhaps he was. In my short acquaintance with him, I discovered I don't care for Lord Warwick. He was most forward."

"Did you discourage him?"

Whatever was Simon about? "Pardon me, my lord, but are you accusing me of something?" Why did he have her feeling as though she'd done something wrong? And who was he to question her anyway?

"No. No, I'm not accusing you of anything. I just wondered how you ended up on the floor with your skirts above your knees in front of a room full of people."

Elise's mouth dropped open and heat rose from her middle. "I fell, my lord. And the reason I fell was because you called my name. Lord Warwick, who was holding my hand against my wishes, let go as I tugged once more, and it threw me off balance. Therefore, I slid from the silk-covered settee." She took in a deep breath. "However, please explain to me how it is that I owe you an account of my behavior."

Simon pulled the gig over to a shady spot on the road and turned to her. "I am sorry. I don't mean to be so imperious. It's just that Warwick has a reputation with the ladies, and I was concerned that he upset you in some way."

She smoothed out the non-existent wrinkles from her gown, then rested her hands in her lap. "He did upset me. However, I feel I had the situation under control." She stuck her finger into his chest. "And tell me, my lord, why were you coughing and nodding, and calling my name? Wasn't the lovely Miss Abbott keeping you busy enough?"

"Her chattering would drive a man to desperate measures. Which was why I wanted you to attend with me. If I am to keep men away from you, I believe part of the bargain should be you keeping the marriage-minded mamas and daughters away from me." He snapped the reins once more.

"Very well," she huffed. "We will now help each

other."

CHAPTER THREE

The following Thursday night, Simon left his horse, Diamond, at the mews behind the Pomeroy townhouse and climbed the stairs to Elise's home. On the way back from Lady Townsend's afternoon call, Elise had told him she was holding one of her soirees and would not be available to attend the musicale at the Ellison home with him this evening.

Since he had listened with blistered ears to more than one Ellison musicale, he was only too happy to pass along his regrets. It had been a last minute decision to see what Elise's "intellectual gatherings" were all about.

He smiled at the now familiar man at the door who directed him to the drawing room. The room was already filled with a number of men and women who were involved in a lively debate. Elise stood at the center of a small knot of people, her arms waving around, her face flushed, her eyes sparkling, as she spoke to the group.

Standing there at the doorway, he watched her in her own environment. This was not the young lady who stumbled through a dance and felt unsure of herself in Society. This woman knew her place in the world. Her audience listened with rapt attention. She turned to offer a comment to a man in front of her and glanced in his direction. She stopped, and her mouth dropped open. Two people in her group turned to regard him. An older man viewed him through his quizzing glass.

She said something to the woman next to her and moved toward him, her hand outstretched. "Lord St. George, how nice of you to join us."

He bent over her hand and kissed it, holding onto it a little too long to be proper. Her face flushed as she tugged it away from him. "Let me introduce you to my guests." She placed her hand on his arm and led him to the group she'd just left. Waving at the people in her group she said, "Miss Henrietta Gordon, Mrs. Jules James, Professor Marvin Lesh, Mr. Joseph Barnes, and Lord Westin, may I present to you the Viscount St. George."

Simon took the ladies' hands and bowed over them, then nodded at the gentlemen. "I am pleased to meet all of you."

The man with the quizzing glass—who turned out to be Lord Westin—said, "Never saw you before at these things, St. George. From what I hear, you're more of the social set than the rest of us are."

"Lady Elise was kind enough to invite me, and I am pleased to be able to join you."

Elise's raised eyebrow was her only reaction to his blatant lie. He had not been invited, most likely since she never thought he would come, but after turning down the invitation to the musicale, he found himself at a loss as to what to do with his evening. Almost as if drawn by an invisible force, he'd found himself riding directly to her home.

After a few minutes of conversation about the latest political ploy by the Whigs, Elise dragged him to another group and made introductions. Those guests were discussing the recently released book, *Prometheus Unbound*, by Shelley. Having not even heard of the book, he kept his mouth shut so as not to show his deficiencies. Elise had quite a bit to say about the tome. Simon was impressed.

Very impressed.

The next group debated the recent discovery of the Venus de Milo on the island of Melos and whether it was authentic. He watched in wonder as again, Elise had an opinion that everyone in the group listened to quite carefully. By the time she announced a light supper would be served, Simon's head was about to burst.

He had never felt so uninformed in his life. As a young man, he had enjoyed his studies at University, and unlike most men of his class, he actually attended lectures and entered into debates with some of the professors who held sessions in their homes in the evenings. Being here tonight brought back those memories and how much he missed them.

Thinking all these people were so well informed and came together on a regular basis to discuss and debate the important issues of the day left him feeling quite jealous that he had not known of their existence.

The guests filled their plates with a variety of foods from the table. Roast duck, creamed trout, pickled celery, apple tarts, and lemon jelly made for an array of tastes. Once he filled plates for himself and Elise, he joined her at a table small enough for just the two of them.

A footman poured wine and placed pots of tea on the tables scattered throughout the room.

Elise shook out her serviette and placed it on her

lap. "What brings you here tonight, my lord?"

He grinned at her. "Ah, perhaps you did not hear me say I had been invited by the illustrious hostess, Lady Elise Smith?"

"Funny, somehow that slipped my mind." She took a bite of duck and licked her lips. Simon's blood all headed south. "I thought you had a musicale to attend this evening."

He wiped his mouth, wishing Elise would do the same and stop licking her lips. "I have attended Ellison musicales for several years and I fear they get no better."

"And you thought my little gathering would be of more interest?"

Of more interest? He could not remember the last time he had been so intellectually stimulated. This "little gathering" of hers made him realize how much time he'd spent discussing inane things with simpering debutantes and boring matrons. The wasted hours spent playing cards at his clubs and arguing over the best horseflesh at Tattersalls.

"Yes. I must admit I find your friends and their conversations quite fascinating. I can say I thoroughly enjoyed myself."

"Indeed? You do not condemn me as a bluestocking?" She tilted her head and gave him a saucy smile.

How could he tell this innocent woman that seeing her in this setting, with the excitement in her eyes as she spoke, had him wanting to throw her over his shoulder and find the nearest bed? A bluestocking, indeed. She was everything the silly women of the *ton* were not.

And that scared the hell out of him.

***

Elise did not like that Simon had enjoyed himself so much. She wanted to continue to think of him as a typical gentleman interested in Society and all the things men of the *ton* did with their time. Relegating him to that part of her life made their association banal. Now he seemed more real, more not-so-easy to dismiss. For some reason, that disturbed her.

"How often do you hold these gatherings?"

Elise placed her fork alongside her plate. "Once a month, but then in addition to that, most of us get together every couple of weeks to attend a lecture or a poetry reading."

Simon looked as though he'd swallowed something nasty. Elise laughed. "I take it lectures and poetry are not to your liking?"

"Lectures, fine. Poetry, no. I can tolerate the ones I can understand, but others leave me wondering what the deuced the author is trying to say. Then some other poems raise questions. For example, why did the mariner shoot the albatross in 'The Rime of the Ancient Mariner'? I've often wondered if the author meant it to be a big joke."

Elise felt her jaw drop. Who was this man? Why was he surprising her so? He should be bored and anxious to leave, eager to scurry away to one of his clubs. Or visit his mistress. He must surely have one. He was unmarried and virile enough to want bed activities on a regular basis.

She flushed at the image that flashed into her mind of both of them naked in bed. A wave of heat started in her stomach and climbed to her face. Hopefully Simon would not notice and mention it.

She also hated how the thought of him in bed

with his mistress disturbed her. They were friends. He was helping her avoid marriage, and she, in turn, was doing the same for him. That was all this relationship was about. Cohorts in crime. When the Season ended, she would convince Papa she was unmarriageable and resume her happy life.

Since she would not return to Society, their paths would never cross again. She must keep that at the forefront. "I must admit, Simon, you are full of surprises tonight."

"Ah, I think you believe I am some sort of fluff who spends his time drinking, racing, gambling, and . . . Well, let's just say the usual proclivities of gentlemen."

She studied him for a moment. "Actually, yes. When you approached Lady Dearborn for an introduction, I had no idea you were a highbrow."

Simon choked. "Now wait a minute, my dear. I am not a frivolous gentleman or a wastrel, but certainly not a highbrow."

She leaned forward, a smirk on her face. Now she would prove to him, and herself, that he was not of her ilk. "Do you speak French, Italian, and German?"

"Fluently."

Her brows drew together. "Familiar with Latin?"

"Yes. Read and write it."

She tapped her finger on the table and offered him a smug look. "Have you heard of, or read, the works of Aristotle, Plato, Voltaire, or Thomas Reid?"

Simon shifted in his chair and ran his finger around the inside of his cravat. "Yes."

She grinned. "Acquainted with the paintings by Benjamin West and Jean-Baptiste-Camille Corot?

Opera? Beethoven, Bach—"

Simon held up his hand. "Stop."

"I believe I have made my point, my lord. Underneath that rakish demeanor lies a highbrow." She sat back and pondered. Why did that not make her happy? She found her admiration for the man increase as he answered all her questions. However, when she thought it over, it would be difficult to dismiss Simon in the future as someone who would never understand her, which had been another strike against marriage.

She was in trouble.

Elise stood as her guests began their departure. It took a while to see them all out, safely in their carriages and on their way. She stood at the entrance hall, waiting for a moment, gathering her thoughts. Simon had remained behind, and that made her a bit nervous.

Simon in a ballroom, in an open carriage, and in a gathering of intellectuals she could handle. Simon alone with her in the quiet house, where everyone else was most likely in their bedchambers, was a different matter.

Stiffening her shoulders and calling herself so much the fool, she returned to the drawing room. Simon stood at the window, staring into the darkness. He turned when she entered.

"I know your step." He walked toward her, slowly, almost like a sleek animal eyeing its prey. "I think it is time for me to leave."

"Yes. I believe so." Her nervousness returned in full force. Something had changed between them, and she wasn't sure she was at all comfortable with it. "I will see you out." She quickly walked to the door and was halfway down the corridor when he reached for her hand, having followed her.

"What?"

He opened the door to the library and drew her in. Leaving the door slightly ajar, he placed his hands on her shoulders and studied her for a minute. Her heart began to pound, and suddenly her legs had a problem holding her up.

"This." His head descended, and his lips almost touched hers. "I have wanted to do this all night." Moving the rest of the way, he drew her into his arms. His mouth covered hers in a way she had never expected. His lips were warm, moist, tasting of wine and tea. At her slight sigh, he wrapped one strong arm around her waist and crushed her body to his.

His other hand cupped the back of her head, moving it in a way that allowed him to take the kiss deeper. He nudged her lips with his tongue and smiled when she opened. She might be an innocent, but she knew that what he was doing to her would lead to something wonderful if she allowed it to continue.

At present she could see no reason why she should stop him. As a bluestocking, she should be open to all sorts of new experiences, and besides that, it felt absolutely wonderful. Not one to shy away, she moved her hands up his back and played with the curls hanging over his cravat.

After a few minutes he pulled away and leaned his forehead against hers. They were both breathing heavily. "Do I need to apologize?"

She stared back at him. "No. Why would you?"

"I had not planned this, I promise. Generally I don't take advantage of innocent young ladies." He drew back and cupped her cheek. "But now I must go before I do something we will both regret."

She had a pretty good idea what he meant, and in some ways she was sorry he'd decided that. In fact, the thought just occurred to her that maybe as part of her spinster, bluestocking experience, she should take a lover. She still had no intention of marrying, so maybe a dalliance with Simon would be just the thing.

"What?" he said.

She smiled. "Nothing, why?"

"You are looking at me with a very odd expression on your face."

She took his arm and walked him to the door. "Good night, my lord."

***

The following afternoon, Lord Pomeroy entered the Earl of Blackwell's townhouse and handed his card to the man at the door. He followed the butler down a corridor to the earl's study. A large, bright room, with windows from the floor to the ceiling, the scant sun shone on a polished wooden desk, with Blackwell sitting behind it. He looked up as Pomeroy entered, pushed aside a ledger, and stood. "Good afternoon, Pomeroy."

"Good to see you, Blackwell."

They shook hands and Blackwell waved to a chair by the fireplace. "Would you care for tea? Or brandy?"

Pomeroy rubbed his hands together. "A bit of brandy would be nice."

Once the two men were settled, Pomeroy took a sip of his brandy and placed the glass on a small table between them. "I am here to ask a favor of you."

"Anything I can do. You know I owe you for

rescuing me from that financial debacle I almost get involved in last year."

"Yes, bad business, bad business. Someone is always out to lighten our pockets and load up theirs." He shook his head at the perfidy of man. "You, of course, know my lovely daughters?"

"Yes. Charming girls. Three, correct?"

"Indeed. The loves of my life. Elise is three and twenty, Juliet nine and ten years, and little Marigold is eight and ten. Love them all. Remind me of their mother, bless her soul." He made the sign of the cross as he always did when he mentioned the late Lady Pomeroy, even though neither of them were Catholic.

"What is it I can help you with?"

"I'd like you to address your suit to Elise."

Blackwell spit out a bit of brandy and coughed enough that Pomeroy found it necessary to step over to the man and clap him several times on the back. Then he poured a glass of water and handed it to him.

His host wiped his eyes with a handkerchief, and took a deep breath, alarm written all over his face. "You are asking me to marry your daughter?"

"No, no. Nothing like that. I want you to pretend to court her."

Blackwell's body visibly relaxed. "Maybe you'd better explain yourself."

"No one is lovelier than my girls. Not a day goes by that I don't thank the good Lord for the blessing of their presence. Also, not a day goes by that a new stack of bills doesn't arrive. Gowns, gloves, slippers, nightgowns, robes, bonnets, fans. I tell you, the list is endless." He stopped for a moment and stared into space, remembering the bills that had just arrived that morning.

Shaking his head, he continued. "My two younger girls will be married in no time. Beautiful faces, lovely forms, charming personalities. They are not the problem. But my dear Elise." He sighed. "She is what is known as a bluestocking. Doesn't like Society, eschews any mention of marriage, and holds what she calls 'intellectual gatherings.' Very strange people show up at these things. I generally ensconce myself in my library until the place clears out."

Pomeroy held up his glass and Blackwell fetched him a refill. "Go on."

I told my lovelies that I would not entertain offers for my two younger girls until Elise married."

"Well. How did she take that?"

"Not well, I'm afraid. Once Lady Pomeroy passed away, Elise took over the mother role for Juliet and Marigold. She would not do anything to hurt their chances at marriage, which is something they dearly desire." He waved his finger "They, you see, are sensible young ladies who know what their duty in life is."

Blackwell nodded.

"Elise has been courted for the past two weeks by a wonderful man, Viscount St. George. Had him checked out. Sober fellow. Doesn't participate in drunken races with his curricle at dawn with the other loons, or toss his inheritance away on games. If the man has a mistress, he's discreet about it."

"Well, if she already has a suitor, why do you need me to pretend to court her?"

"When a man has daughters and no wife to supervise them, he has to find ways to discover what the devil they're up to." He took a sip of brandy.

"Consequently, I listen at doors, and you would be surprised what women will discuss without being sure they are not overheard. My lovely, intelligent, devious eldest daughter has conspired with St. George to have him pretend to court her to keep the other bucks away, and then at the end of the Season he will hie off to the country.

"The plan is for my poor, brokenhearted daughter to tell me she is unmarriageable and we should just allow Juliet and Marigold to have their Season and find husbands."

Blackwell let out with the low whistle. "Very clever."

"Yes. Very clever, indeed." He sat morosely, looking at his glass. "But," he perked up, "I have a plan." He moved to the edge of the chair. "I will introduce you to Elise as a man who has approached me about accepting his suit. I will tell her if no one else offers for her, I will accept your offer."

"I assume you hope St. George comes up to scratch when he sees competition?"

"Exactly. I think these two will do very well together. He actually attended one of her gatherings last night and did not run screaming from the house. Either he is one of these intellectuals himself, or he is fond of Elise."

"What is your guess?"

Pomeroy drank the last of his brandy and smiled. "As I say, when you have daughters you have to find ways to learn what they are up to. As always, last night I hid during Elise's gathering, and when St. George was taking his leave, he pulled her into my library. It was dark, and they never saw me just sitting there, enjoying the solitude."

"And?"

"And let's just say I don't believe young St. George is as much of a *pretend* suitor as Elise believes. One little nudge and he will be right where I want him." He pointed at Blackwell. "You, my lord, are that nudge."

CHAPTER FOUR

"You sent for me, Papa?" Elise tugged on her gloves as she entered her father's study.

He looked up from the newspaper he read. "Yes, my darling girl. I have some excellent news for you." He pointed to a chair in front of his desk, then walked around the desk and leaned his hip on the edge, his foot swinging back and forth. This was another of those times when she realized how young and very handsome her father was.

He was only five and forty years, and even though that seemed like a great age to her, she'd seen ladies looking at him when he attended a social event or two. He was always inundated with invitations, but accepted very few.

His brown hair had light streaks of gray throughout, but his face was strong, with only crinkles at the edge of his eyes and near his mouth. His blue eyes oftentimes twinkled with humor. Yes, it was a mystery as to why he'd remained single all these years. Since Mother had been his great love, he seemed to want no other.

Then a frightening thought crossed her mind. Was this plan of Papa's a way to get rid of all three of them so he could marry again? Goodness, a new wife would certainly not want another woman running the household. Disturbing notion, that.

"What is your great news, Papa?"

"I have found a husband for you."

She reared back as if he'd slapped her. All the air left her lungs, and for a moment black dots danced in front of her eyes. Surely she'd misheard him? "A husband?"

"Yes." He rubbed his hands together. "'Tis all taken care of. Now you don't have to worry about bringing young St. George up to scratch."

"But…but…I like Simon. I mean, St. George." Whatever was Papa doing now? She had to dissuade him from this plan. She had her own plan.

"Ah, here is Lord Blackwell now." Her father moved toward the door and shook hands with an older man. He looked a bit unsure of himself as he entered the room and cast an uneasy glance in her direction. He seemed of an age with her father. Even though she had just been thinking how young and handsome Papa was, she certainly didn't want to consider a man of that age for herself!

Wait just a minute. She didn't want to consider *any* man for herself. Good grief, her perfect plan was falling apart.

"My dear, may I present to you the Earl of Blackwell." He smiled warmly at her, and then said, "Blackwell, this is my eldest darling daughter, Lady Elise Smith." He looked back and forth between them as if planning the menu for the wedding breakfast.

Drawing on years of good manners, she extended her arm and allowed Blackwell to take her hand and then bow to her. "My lady, your servant."

She curtsied. "My lord, it is nice to meet you."

Oh, God, how could she get out of this? Lord Blackwell appeared to be a nice man. Pleasant looking, and nice eyes, but she had no intention of marrying him.

"My lady, I have been invited to Lady Townsend's garden party two days hence. I would consider it an honor if you deign to accompany me."

Why did she think he had memorized those words? They came out very stilted. Also, he looked over to Papa, almost for approval.

Papa slapped Blackwell on the back. "Of course, she will. My sweet girl loves garden parties, don't you, my dear?" He looked at her with such love and devotion she felt a slight pang of guilt at the duplicity in which she and Simon were engaged. Then she told herself Papa was manipulating her like he'd never done before. That gave her pause. She would not give up or give in.

With both men staring at her, she had no choice at this point. "Yes, my lord, I would love to attend Lady Townsend's garden party with you."

"I look forward to it. I will be by about two o'clock." Blackwell bowed and turned to her father. "Pomeroy, I wonder if I might have a word with you in private."

Elise was more than happy to escape the room. She did a quick dip and hurried away. Once she was outside the study, she took a deep breath and leaned against the wall. This was a mess. She had to send word to Simon of Papa's plan. It was his job to keep men away, and it appeared he needed to increase his attentions to convince Papa.

***

The ride to Lady Townsend's garden party was quiet.

Lord Blackwell was gracious and attentive, but she couldn't help but feel something was off. He certainly did not act like a man who had approached her father for the purpose of presenting his suit. Until he appeared in Papa's study, she'd never laid eyes on the man. Where had he seen her, that he decided he wanted to court her?

They rolled up to the townhouse, along with several other carriages, also alighting passengers. Blackwell jumped out of the carriage and turned to help her out. She took his hand, thinking how different it felt from Simon's. Blackwell smiled at her, but somehow it didn't quite reach his eyes.

A footman stood on the pavement and directed the guests to follow the path alongside the townhouse, which took them to the back garden area. Guests wandered around, some chatting with other guests, some admiring the flower gardens. Tables had been set up, and footmen carried trays of lemonade.

"Would you enjoy a stroll, my lady? Or would you prefer to greet some of the guests?"

What she wanted was to go home and read the book she'd started that morning. At least when she was with Simon, he kept her entertained with humorous repartee and amusing comments about other guests that had her biting the inside of her cheek to keep from laughing.

"Lady Elise, I had no idea you would be here this afternoon." Her heart sped up at the sound of Simon's voice. She turned, and her breath caught. The sun glistened on his hair, highlighting the red streaks. His blue eyes sparkled as he bowed to her. Snug breeches tucked into shiny Hessian boots, covered his muscled thighs. His dark brown jacket and tan and silver waistcoat, topped off with a rakishly tied cravat completed the perfect outfit for a lordly gentleman at an afternoon garden party.

Of course he'd been fully aware that she was attending the garden party and with whom. She'd sent a note as soon as she had escaped to her room, right after leaving Papa and Lord Blackwell. Besides telling him of Papa's plan, she chastised him for not doing a proper job of keeping men away.

But then, in all honesty, she had to admit even she had no idea from whence Lord Blackwell had come to offer his attentions. Strange, that.

"Good afternoon, my lord." She gave him a slight curtsey, then turned to Blackwell. "Lord Blackwell, may I make known to you Viscount St. George?" She paused. "My lord, may I introduce the Earl of Blackwell?"

Both men bowed and eyed each other with such scrutiny Elise almost laughed out loud. They looked like dogs circling a meaty bone.

"My lord!" A voice shattered the low hum of conversation and drove a shudder though Elise's body. Miss Abbott hurried up to them, her plain face pinched with annoyance. She took Simon's arm and, smoothing out the frown on her face, smiled brightly. "I hadn't realized you arrived." She tapped him on the arm with her fan. "I thought you would come find me."

"I am sorry, my lady, please forgive me. However, I have only just now arrived."

Elise nearly snorted at the false words spewing from Simon's mouth. She looked back and forth at Blackwell and Miss Abbott. Neither one of them realized the insincerity of his words. Didn't they hear the artifice in his voice?

Apparently not.

"Good afternoon, my lord, my lady," Miss Abbott said to Blackwell and Elise, tugging Simon's arm even closer. "I am so glad you were able to join us for our little party."

Miss Abbott then spent five minutes reciting all the things necessary for one to put on a "little event," as she called the garden party. To hear her tell it, she had personally visited the markets to buy the food, cooked it, decorated the garden, and hauled the tables from inside the house to the patio area, instead of all those jobs being done by servants.

She looked up at Simon, batting her eyelashes. "Would you care to take a stroll in the garden?"

Simon looked as though he was headed to the executioner. He glared at Elise, the silent message being that she was supposed to be protecting him from any situation that Miss Abbott maneuvered him into that might result in the parson's noose.

"What a wonderful idea, Miss Abbott." Elise turned to Blackwell. "Shall we join them, my lord?"

Blackwell looked surprised, as if he wasn't even sure what a stroll, or even a garden, was. "Yes, of course. That is a lovely idea." He held his arm out, and Elise took it.

"How nice of you to join us," Miss Abbot said, looking as though she'd found a nasty piece of business on the bottom of her shoe.

Elise grinned a smile as insincere as she could make it. Simon rolled his eyes.

The four of them descended the patio steps to the garden and began their stroll.

***

Simon would never get enough of watching Elise's body as she walked with Blackwell in front of him and Miss Abbott. The gentle sway of her hips, the curls that fell from her topknot caught by the light breeze, her long, slender neck, the melodious sound of her voice as she conversed with Blackwell.

Damn the man.

Simon was still stunned by the turn of events. He'd thought he and Pomeroy had gotten on quite well the couple of times they'd spoken, so why would he bring in someone else as a potential husband for Elise? And why did that bother him so much? Of course, he told himself, it merely meant he had not held up his end of their deal—keeping men away from her. That was all, nothing else. He'd let her down.

It frightened him to think it meant more than that. He'd sworn since he was ten years old and his mother had abandoned him and his father to run off with a lover that he would never marry. His father had spent the rest of his days sitting in his library, drinking. That only lasted a year until he rode out one night and was thrown from his horse and broke his neck. Simon knew it had not been an accident. The man had given up on life. A lesson well-learned for an eleven-year-old boy: Don't allow anyone to have that much control over your feelings.

Because of his mother's treachery, he'd been left an orphan and titleholder at a very young age. No carefree childhood for him. If his mother had ever learned of her husband's death, he did not know. He'd never seen her again, and no one had ever mentioned her to him. He believed the family solicitors had attempted to find her but were unsuccessful. The last he'd heard, she was in Italy.

While he ruminated on the problem of what to do about Blackwell, Miss Abbott's shrill voice prattled on about some nonsense having to do with the correct ribbon to match a gown. The entire monologue was making him itchy. Thank God Blackwell and Elise had agreed to walk with them. He could only imagine Miss Abbott—or her mother—conniving to have them caught in a compromising positon with all the guests at the garden party as witnesses.

He shuddered to think of a life listening to her jarring voice every single day. At least his heart would not be in danger.

Just his ears and sanity.

They continued their walk, the meandering path bringing them back to the rest of the party. Simon managed to shake off Miss Abbott's arm when her mother called to her. He immediately made his way over to Blackwell and Elise. "My lady, may I have a word with you?"

Elise turned to Blackwell. "Do you mind, my lord?"

The older man assured them it was perfectly fine with him. An odd smile graced his face, which Simon dismissed. Blackwell wandered to the table against the balustrade, perusing the variety of foods.

Simon escorted Elise away from the general crowd, making sure they stayed in sight, but not where they could be overheard. "What the devil is going on?"

Elise whispered furiously. "I have no idea. You were supposed to keep other men away."

"That was precisely what I was doing. Your

father seemed pleased when we spoke," Simon shot back. "How did all of this come about?"

Elise looked at the other guests and leaned in, lowering her voice. "Papa called me to his study two days ago and told me he'd found a husband for me. Before I could even grasp that information, Blackwell showed up. The next thing I knew, Papa had accepted the invitation for this garden party on my behalf."

"I thought we agreed we would attend together," he snapped. Realizing how possessive that sounded, he added, "Because, you know, you were supposed to protect me from Miss Abbott."

Elise stuck her finger into his chest. "If you want my help with that ninny-hammer, *you* have to find a way to get rid of Blackwell."

He huffed. "What shall I do, kiss you senseless right here in front of everyone?"

His breath hitched at the look on Elise's face. The anger was still there, but somehow had segued into something strangely resembling passion. Her eyes darkened, and she licked her lips. Both of them were breathing heavily.

Bloody hell, why had he said that? Now all he could think about was how sweet she'd tasted. How soft and warm her lips had been. How her mouth tasted of tea and Elise, and how her body pressed to his had felt exactly right. All the blood that had been pounding in his head since she and Blackwell had arrived immediately took a journey south.

"No," she said, her voice raspy, "of course, I don't expect you to do that." She continued to stare at him with a look that said she wished for the exact opposite of her words.

"My lord, we've decided to play Pall Mall. I have

already claimed you as my partner." Miss Abbot's strident voice broke whatever spell Elise had cast on him. The chit walked up to them and linked her arm into his. "Lady Elise, I am sure you and *your escort*, Lord Blackwell, will wish to join us."

Elise shook her head as if clearing it. "Yes. That sounds like just the thing." She made a quick dip in his direction. "If you will excuse me, my lord." She hurried away from him, taking all the sunlight with her.

Damnation!

CHAPTER FIVE

There were a total of four couples for the Pall Mall game. It was decided Blackwell and Simon and their partners would team up to play against Mr. Woodward, Lord Appleton, and their partners.

Although Elise had not spent much time on Society foolery, she'd played quite a few games in the country with her sisters. Pall Mall was one of her favorite games, and she was good, as well as fiercely competitive. She picked her mallet and ball, and returned to Blackwell's side. "Are you familiar with the game, my lord?"

"Yes. I have played a number of times. I won't say I'm the best at it, but I do think I will not disgrace us."

"Good." Elise nodded. "I have played the game for years."

He smiled at her. "We should acquit ourselves quite well, then."

The two teams gathered, a coin was tossed, and their team went first.

"I think we should allow the ladies first crack at it," Blackwell said. He nodded in Miss Abbott's direction. "Miss Abbott, you may start."

"Oh, dear. Now that I have suggested this game,

I am not certain how to stand or hold the mallet." She giggled and looked in Simon's direction. Elise gritted her teeth and rolled her eyes.

Simon sighed and walked up to her, placing her hands in the correct position on the mallet. He did not stand behind and wrap his arms around her, which Elise was grateful for. "Do you know what the object of the game is?"

"Yes. I think it is to knock the ball through those little loop things." She looked up at him and batted her eyelashes.

Elise mumbled something very unladylike under her breath, and Blackwell grinned.

The addlebrained woman barely tapped the ball. It rolled no more than a few inches. "Oh, dear. That's not good, is it?"

"We're never going to win with her on our team." Elise said it low enough that only Blackwell heard her. He nodded. "I'm afraid so."

Simon looked over at her when she growled. "Lady Elise, you are next."

She stomped up and told herself to calm down. She had the desire to whack the ball so hard it would land on Bond Street, but that would not help her team. Taking a deep breath, she hit the ball with just enough force to send it right through the first hoop.

"Well done!" Lord Blackwell said.

Simon gave her a short salute.

Miss Abbott annoyed everyone with her whining voice. "Oh, I'm afraid Lady Elise is so much more athletic than I am."

C'est la vérité.

Simon was next and also put his ball through the hoop.

"Oh, how wonderful, my lord. You are such an excellent team member," Miss Abbott panted.

Elise felt the need to whack the woman over her head with her mallet.

Blackwell stepped up next and got close to the hoop, a few inches shy.

"Oh, dear, everyone is so much better than me."

Oh, that voice.

"Perhaps you would prefer to sit the game out, Miss Abbott, since you are so unaccustomed to *athletic* events." Elise looked around. "I am sure there is a tree somewhere you could sit underneath. I have no doubt the three of us will be able to win against the other team while you rest."

Miss Abbott's drawn-in breath and Simon's choking sound brought Elise a bit of satisfaction.

Miss Abbott glared at her with steely eyes. This woman might play the soft fluff-head, but she was a worthy opponent. Good. Elise was in the mood for the challenge.

It amazed Elise how improved Miss Abbot's skills became after their little confrontation. The men watched with mounting amusement as the two women hacked at their balls. Elise drove Miss Abbott's ball into the pond. She, in turn, propelled Elise's into a flowerbed that had Lady Townsend screeching about her flowers.

They both ignored her as they glared at each other and took aim.

Elise hit her ball hard enough to knock Miss Abbott's into the shrubbery. Undaunted, the girl climbed into the bushes and smacked her ball into Elise's leg. Elise ignored the pain and limped to the next loop. On her way, she stepped on Miss Abbott's ball, sinking it a couple of inches into the soft ground

When Miss Abbott stood to hit her ball, she took out tufts of grass in her enthusiasm to cuff her ball. The team they were supposed to be playing against had fallen far behind. No one was even keeping score. Each round became more contentious until Simon pulled Elise aside and said, "Maybe we should calm down a bit."

She tugged her elbow free. "This isn't a game, my lord. This is war."

Elise whacked her ball, and it flew through the final hoop, striking a tree. It ricocheted off, smacking Lord Howell in the back of the head, where he sat speaking with Lady Miller. The man slumped to the ground.

Elise held her mallet in the air and whooped.

Miss Abbot pushed Elise aside, almost knocking her to the ground, and walloped her ball right through the final hoop, sending it over the garden fence to smash a window on the townhouse next door. She raised her chin and regarded Elise.

"I believe it is a draw, my lady."

Once Elise and Miss Abbot apologized for the damage they had done, a very rattled Lady Townsend announced there would be music, and the guests were invited to dance if they wished. Since the space was small, and Elise was still feeling restless from the game, she asked Blackwell to walk with her in the garden again.

"My lady, the orchestra has advised me the third number will be a waltz. May I have the pleasure of that dance?" Simon grinned, apparently still amused by the game she and Miss Abbott had just finished. Perhaps he found it humorous they hadn't resorted to hair pulling and rolling on the ground. After all, she was still a lady.

Blackwell nodded at her. "Please feel free to accept Lord St. George's request. Surely we will be back from our stroll by then."

A cotillion started up and Miss Abbott hurried over to them, her obvious intention to capture Simon for the first dance. Elise would enjoy a waltz with Simon. She told herself it was merely because if he was waltzing with her, he would not be waltzing with Miss Abbott. "Yes, my lord, I would enjoy a waltz."

She and Blackwell made their way into the garden. He was truly a very nice man, had not chastised her for her behavior during the game, and seemed eager to please her, whether it was a stroll in the garden or a dance with another gentleman. He would make someone a very nice husband.

Just not her.

As they returned from their walk and approached the patio, the waltz started up. Simon walked slowly toward her, a slight smile on his face, holding out his hand. She looked into his eyes and something there had her lady parts sitting up and singing a serenade. Her nipples grew hard, and a slight shudder ran through her. Her heart sped up and she felt flushed, almost as if she were suffering a fever. She placed her hand in his, and the feelings only grew stronger.

They walked to the area set aside for dancing, and he swung her into his arms. "Lady Elise, who knew a bluestocking such as yourself was so competitive?" His eyes flashed with humor, and his grin had her smiling back.

His warm hand on her lower back heated the spot right through his glove. "I do not like to lose, my lord."

"So it appeared." He leaned in closer, even though some of the older ladies might be scandalized. "You have quite the temper. I wonder how many other ways you might release that fury."

She licked her lips, her mouth suddenly dry. "I am not sure I know what you mean."

"Ah, yes you do. You are far too intelligent to not know of what I speak."

If her heart beat any louder it would drown out the music. "Should I be outraged? Should I slap your face?"

His eyes grew sultry. "Do you want to?" he whispered, and pulled her too close for propriety. She moved in slightly to press her breasts against his coat. Simon sucked in a breath and his nostrils flared. "Be careful, my lady, you are playing with fire."

"Who says I'm playing?"

He drew in in air through his teeth. "We must stop this now, or I will not be able to walk away from the dance area without disgracing myself. Now behave yourself." He loosened his grip and she moved back, a smirk on her face.

They finished the dance, and he returned her to Blackwell since Miss Abbott was reminding him he owed her a dance. He bowed. "Thank you, my lady."

Blackwell touched her elbow. "Would you care for another dance?"

"No. In fact, if you don't mind, I believe I would like to leave. I find the sun has given me a slight headache."

"Of course." He extended his arm and she laid

her fingers there. They approached Lady Townsend and thanked her. The hostess eyed Elise with disdain, but said nothing untoward. Blackwell requested one of the footmen to have his carriage brought around.

Once they were away from the noise of the crowd and the distraction of Simon, Elise relaxed. Her feelings and emotions were troubling her. She'd never before in her life felt the things she did with Simon. Her body still felt alive, but prickly at the same time, as if she was missing something.

She felt as though her clothes were scratching her skin and constricting her. There was a definite dampness between her legs, and she had an overpowering urge to push that part of her body against something hard.

Whatever was happening to her? While she knew all about passion, she had never experienced it and was afraid it was the dance with Simon that had brought this all about. There was no doubt all these sensations and feelings would be assuaged by his attentions.

Again she thought it might be a good idea to take him as a lover. They were both intelligent, mature adults. Neither wanted anything as permanent as marriage. How would she go about suggesting it? Did one simply walk up to the man and say *I would like you to be my lover, my lord. What say you?*

Maybe that *was* the way to do it.

***

Simon dropped the knocker against the door to the Pomeroy townhouse. The butler greeted him with friendliness and said, "Lady Elise will be down momentarily. His lordship requests that you join him in his study."

He followed the butler to the study, where he found Pomeroy busy at his desk. He looked up and waved Simon in. “Come in, my boy. So good to see you. Have a seat.” He spoke to the butler. “Have Cook send in coffee and rolls.”

Simon took a seat and waited to see what Pomeroy was about. Hopefully he wasn’t preparing to tell him Elise was betrothed to Blackwell. He quelled the panic that thought brought on.

“So, you and my lovely daughter are off for a ride this morning?” Pomeroy walked around the desk and sat on the edge, swinging his foot.

“Yes, sir. Off to Rotten Row.”

“Good, good. Lovely day for it, too.”

Simon looked out the window at the threatening rain. Despite the risk of getting wet, he’d decided to call on Elise for their ride anyway. Since the garden party three days ago, he’d thought of nothing else but getting Elise alone to see just how far she would let him go. If the look in her eye at the Townsend party was telling, she seemed ready to venture into territory he could easily lead her. What that meant for their future he had no idea and did not want to think much on it.

“Wonderful girl, Lady Elise.” Pomeroy brought him back to the present.

“Yes, sir.” What the devil was the man up to now? He’d just announced to Elise only a few days ago that he was going to pass her off to Blackwell. While quite fond of Lord Pomeroy, he certainly found him confusing.

“I just wanted to let you know how much I appreciate you squiring Lady Elise around. It’s good for her to go out in Society. She’s always avoided it, you know."

"Yes, sir. I am aware that she does not favor *ton* events."

Get to the point, man.

"I guess you wonder why I invited you in talk."

"Yes, I am curious."

"My daughter, for all her bluster, is soft and tender on the inside. I would not like to see her heart broken. As much as I would like to witness all my daughters happily married and settled in their own homes, I will not abide anyone causing them pain on their path to the altar."

What the hell?

"I agree, sir. I would not like to see anyone cause Lady Elise pain." This was by far the most convoluted conversation he'd had in a long time. He wasn't precisely sure what it was Pomeroy was trying to tell him, but he began to sweat anyway. He thought Blackwell was the chosen one. Now he had no idea.

"Oh, there you are." Elise came into the study, adjusting her hat, dressed for her ride. His mouth watered at the sight. She wore a pale blue riding habit with black piping that fit her fine form like a well-used glove. The silly little hat sat on top of her head, a feather curving toward her mouth. Plump lips. She smiled and he grinned back.

After a few moments Pomeroy cleared his throat, and they both looked at him. "Have a nice ride."

"Yes. Right." Simon placed his hand on Elise's lower back and they left the room. The horses were ready and waiting for them when they descended the stairs. Elise glanced up at the sky. "It appears our ride might be cut short."

"Hopefully we can get it in before the skies open

up." He lifted her onto the saddle, his hands lingering on her waist, as well as a bit lower, for a moment. She blushed and fussed with her skirts, making sure they covered her legs.

They headed toward Hyde Park and then onto Rotten Row, the broad track running along the south side of the park, leading from Hyde Park Corner to Serpentine Road. Apparently most early morning riders had decided to forego a ride, based on the weather, which was fine with Simon since it left the track almost empty.

They rode, side by side, for about twenty minutes when the first raindrops fell. Elise looked over at him. "Should we make a run for it?"

Simon looked up and was rewarded with a splash on his face. "Let's move over to that cluster of trees. Perhaps it will pass in a little while."

Once they were safe under the trees, Simon jumped from his horse, tied the reins to a branch, then placed his hands around Elise's waist. She stared at him as he slowly lowered her, sliding her body against his. Once she was on her feet, her hands resting on his shoulders, she licked her lips, her sweet earnest eyes meeting his.

He was lost.

With a slight moan, he covered her lips and crushed her body to his. His caress was a command, a way to possess her, and he wanted her to know, and accept. Both of his hands gripped her hair, turning her head to take the kiss where he wanted to go, where he would conquer her. He nudged her lips, demanding acceptance.

She opened, and his tongue explored the warmth and moistness, the sweetness of her breath. He drew back, panting heavily, then rested his forehead against hers. "This is killing me, sweetheart."

"We should do something about that." She studied his lips when she spoke, unable to look him in the eye.

His hold on her tightened and all sorts of images flooded his mind while his blood flooded his cock. She could not possibly mean what he thought she meant. Could she? "What do you mean?"

"I have been thinking. If I am to remain a spinster my whole life, why should I not experience passion?"

He lost his ability to speak as he stared at her. She did mean what he thought she meant. He wanted to shout and run for the nearest bedroom, but then sanity prevailed. "My love, you cannot mean that. You are an innocent, a gently reared woman. You must save yourself for your husband."

She puffed out a breath of air. "How many times do I need to tell you there will be no husband? I intend to never marry. But just because I don't want to be shackled in marriage doesn't mean I need to remain a virgin my entire life."

He closed his eyes, trying very hard to continue the conversation while his cock was shouting its approval so loudly. "Elise, once your give away your maidenhead, there is no turning back."

"I know." She fingered his cravat, still staring at his throat.

"Honey, if you can't even look me in the eye, then I know you're not serious and don't really know what you're saying."

She raised her chin, her eyes sparkling. "Oh, I know exactly what I'm saying and I've given it a lot of thought." She kissed his jaw. "I want to know where all these feelings I get when you kiss me will lead. When I leave you I always feel restless and my clothes feel scratchy and tight."

Once more his mouth covered hers hungrily. She wrapped her arms around his waist, under his jacket, her hands running up and down his back. His hands moved to cup her bottom, pulling against his erection. He released her lips, kissing the pulsing hollow at the base of her throat. Her head fell back and she moaned. He brought his hand around and cupped her breast. Instinctively her body arched into his touch. "Yes."

Oh, God, yes. And yes. And yes.

Luckily sensibility prevailed when he realized they were standing out in the open—despite being under a copse of trees—and they might not be the only riders who decided to wait out the rain by sheltering under the heavy branches.

He pulled away and placed his lips against her temple. "Sweetheart, we can't do this here. Someone could come by and you will be ruined." He pulled away, keeping her at arms' length. "We will have to try to make it to your house."

Looking completely dazed, she nodded and he turned her toward her horse and lifted her up. "Sweetheart, grab your reins and pay attention."

She nodded again.

"Elise!"

"What?"

"You will fall off your horse if you don't pay attention."

She seemed to pull herself together. "I'm fine." She smiled. "Truly, I'm fine."

He vaulted onto his horse, and they both rode into the rain that had now turned into a slight drizzle. By the time they reached the townhouse, they were both wet. He helped her down again as a groom came from the mews and took her horse.

"Do you want to come in and dry off?" she said.

"No. I will go ahead on home." He stopped and looked at her. Her face was still flushed and her lips swollen. Hopefully her father would not see her before she made it to her bedchamber.

She moved closer to him, and standing on tiptoe whispered in his ear. "Come to me tonight. I will leave the back door unlocked. My bedroom is the third one on the right. Papa is always in bed well before midnight."

With that declaration, she turned and hurried up the stairs, leaving him staring at her stupidly.

CHAPTER SIX

Elise paced in her bedroom, the gown she wore flying out as she turned and strode back and forth. It was twenty minutes past midnight. Would he come? She was so sure he would that she had asked Charlene to brush her hair until it shone and rested like a silky curtain around her shoulders.

Once the maid left, Elise removed the gown Charlene had selected for her and dug into her wardrobe for the scanty night rail and matching dressing gown she had purchased last year, just to have something risqué in her wardrobe. She'd never worn it before, but it seemed this would be the best night to do so.

Her heart stopped when she heard a light scratch at her door. She flew to the door and threw it open. Reaching out, she grabbed Simon's hand and dragged him into the room. He turned and locked the door.

Simon was casually dressed in a dark blue jacket and tight breeches, with no waistcoat or cravat. Curly dark hair peeked out from where his shirt opened at his throat. He leaned against the door, studying her, his arms behind his back. "I don't think this is a good idea."

"Then why did you come?" She remained where she was, even though she wanted to throw herself into his arms and once again experience the feelings as when he'd kissed her the way he had that morning.

"I'm a fool, that's why. I couldn't stay away." He pushed himself off the door and dropped his hands, walking toward her stealthily, moving like a sleek beast of the jungle. He stopped right in front of her, no more than six inches away. "You are sure?"

"Yes."

His hand covered her cheek and slowly he drew her to him. He kissed her gently, unlike his other kisses. He released her mouth and placed his lips on her temple. "If you change your mind at any time, just say so and we will stop."

"I won't change my mind."

"Promise."

She stood on tiptoes and kissed the hollow of his throat, then rubbed her nose in the scratchy dark hair. He smelled of mint and soap. "I promise."

"In that case, you are far too dressed, my lady." He slid his large, warm hands under her dressing gown, and, with a quick movement, pushed it off her shoulders to slither to the floor. Wrapping his arm around her waist, he tugged her to him and took her mouth in a kiss reminiscent of the ones he'd given her before.

This.

This was what she wanted. To be crushed to him, to feel the hardness of his body against hers, minus all the underclothing and stays. The tingles once again in her breasts and between her legs had her blood soaring through her body, causing her heart to pound. He moved his mouth to her neck, where he kissed and licked.

She didn't know how he did it, but she felt her

nightgown slither to the floor to join the dressing gown. Had he given her enough time to think about it, she might have been embarrassed at being naked, with him fully clothed. Then, for some reason, the thought of her with no clothes while Simon was dressed excited her further.

Whatever was she turning into?

Simon placed his hands at her waist and lifted her. "Wrap your legs around me."

She complied, and they stared into each other's eyes for a moment. His eyes had darkened to almost black. A slow smile started on his lips, then he bent his head to take one of her breasts in his mouth, suckling softly, then pulling much harder.

Elise drew in a sharp breath as a wave of incredible sensations moved through her body. She threw her head back, his strong hands spanning her back as he gripped her, keeping her from falling backward. He released one breast only to offer the same attention to the other one. Elise moaned as he scraped his teeth over her nipple. With one final lick, he moved his mouth back up to hers. He shifted her so he carried her in his arms to the bed where he laid her down gently, coming down on top of her.

His clothes scratched against her sensitive skin. She rubbed her nipples against his chest, wanting to continue the sensations he'd elicited with his mouth. To her dismay, he sat up, taking all the warmth and heaviness with him. He removed his jacket, then stared at her, his eyes going from her hair, down her body to her toes. A slight flush rose in her at being so closely regarded.

"You are breathtakingly beautiful, Elise. I could spend hours kissing every inch of your body." He ran his large palm over her, dipping into her curves and shaping and massaging her breasts.

"Take off your shirt. I want to feel your skin." The words she whispered brought a flare to Simon's nostrils and a slight smile to his lips. With a swift movement he tugged his shirt from his breeches and pulled it over his head, tossing it to the floor.

His flesh was golden in the candlelight, all powerful muscles and sinew. Instinctively, she raised her hand and ran her palm over his chest, the ripple of muscles, the hardness of his chest, and the sprinkling of dark hair running down the center to end at the waistband of his breeches. Still locking eyes with her, he bent and removed his boots and stockings, then stretched out alongside her, shifting to his side to face her.

"Do you wish to continue?" He smoothed the hair back from her face.

"Move than ever."

He groaned and, resting his warm palm on her hip, tugged her closer. His mouth covered hers with an intensity that raised the heat in her body to a smoldering fire. At last she would have a way to assuage the raw desire she felt whenever he kissed her.

***

Simon had tried his best to make sure Elise knew what she was doing. So far, she'd followed him step-for-step to where he led her. Her innocent, but enthusiastic responses so far had been more of an aphrodisiac than what the most experienced courtesan employed. In some ways she was adorable; in others, a true seductress calling to him in a way he'd never before experienced.

He'd literally lost his breath when he'd entered her room and saw her in night clothes, obviously waiting for him. With her hair cascading over her slender shoulders, resting against her plump breasts, his mouth watered to place his lips there. But the moment he'd laid her down on the bed and seen her completely nude with the candlelight casting her dips and curves into shadows, he'd known were she to withdraw her consent it would be agony for him.

She was part innocence, part temptress. Her ingenuous gaze turned sultry after a few kisses, and his reaction to her gentle touches to his chest brought a siren's smile to her lips. While he gazed at her, his palm wandered over her luscious body. She made low mewing sounds that were driving him crazy. The air surrounding them was filled with the scent of their passion.

At his whispered request, she parted her legs. She was already wet and swollen. Stifling a groan, he leaned in and kissed her mouth, nudging her lips to open to him. Using his finger at her opening and his tongue in her mouth, he mimicked what his cock was screaming to do. He jolted when he felt her fingers fumbling at his falls, apparently attempting to open the buttons.

Simon moved her hand away and, with years of practice, had the flap opened in seconds. He edged back and slid his breeches down, over his hips and down his legs, kicking them free. Elise stared at his cock in wonderment, then reached out and took it in her hand. He hissed as her warm palm wrapped around it.

Moving his mouth to her breasts, he covered one plump mound as her hand squeezed and brought a groan from him. "Like this, sweetheart," he murmured. He placed his hand over hers and moved it up and down, closing his eyes at the sensation.

"It feels strange to me." She grinned at him, a devilish sparkle in her eyes. He loved those eyes. They said everything. There was no guile in Elise. And just like everything else he'd witnessed so far, she brought that honesty to the bedchamber. Used to years with opera dancers and women of the demimonde, to now see genuine responses, and know they were real and not practiced for the purpose of simply pleasing a man, raised the level of his desire.

Since she seemed so responsive and willing to experience pleasure, he kissed his way down her body, dipping his tongue into her belly button, eliciting a giggle from her and bringing a smile to his face. Never had he laughed during sex, a new occurrence, and something that added to his enjoyment with this woman.

He continued down until he reached the dark curls surrounding her feminine sweetness. Widening her legs, he placed his mouth on her nether lips and kissed her slick folds.

"Oh, yes. Oh, Simon, that feels wonderful." She sucked in a breath. "Don't stop."

He had no intention of stopping, having too much fun tasting her warm, moist honey. The scent of her desire surrounded him, bringing him so close to the brink he had to conjugate Latin verbs to keep from climaxing.

His eyes traveled up her body, past the slight swell of her belly, her plump breasts with rosy nipples tight and pert, to her beautiful face. The frown on her forehead told him she was close to release. Her legs tightened, and her panting increased. He felt her muscles constrict as he continued to watch her face. She inhaled deeply and a low keening sound came from her sweet lips. Her body jerked and her knees gripped his shoulders as she thrashed and moaned.

Once her muscles relaxed, he placed his hands on either side of her body and moved up between her open legs to capture her mouth with his, knowing she tasted her own pleasure on his lips. It was a heady feeling, knowing how open she was, how willing to experience everything he had to offer.

"That was wonderful. I've never felt anything like that in my life," she gasped.

He kissed her eyelids, cheeks, and jaw. "Even better than your intellectual gatherings?"

"Oh, yes. A hundred times yes."

Braced on his elbows, he smoothed the damp curls from her forehead and stared at her. "I must ask once again if you are sure about this, Elise. Once 'tis done there is no turning back."

"I am sure."

Thank you, God.

"I'm told this will hurt at first, but hopefully not too much, and I will take it slow." Inch by slow inch he moved into her opening until his cock came up against her maidenhead, something he had never experienced before. It gave him a feeling of caring and possessiveness to be the first man to ever take her completely, to enter her body. That would have frightened him had he given himself time to dwell on it.

In anticipation of any noise she might make, he covered her lips with his when he thrust forward. A slight squeak and a brief tightening of her muscles was her only reaction. Being inside her, feeling her warmth and moistness, knowing no other man had ever experienced this with her, was truly a heady feeling.

He watched her carefully as he moved slightly. "Are you well?"

"Yes." One small tear trickled down her cheek. He removed it with his thumb and rested his forehead on hers. "I will give you a moment to allow your body to adjust."

"There is more?"

He chuckled, the second time he'd experienced humor in bed with Elise. He was feeling all sorts of emotions that he'd never experienced before. Exhilarating in some ways and terrifying in others. But he'd always known sex with Lady Elise Smith would be unlike any other coupling he'd experienced.

When she looked confused at his laughter, he added, "Oh, yes, darling, there is more. If things work correctly, what you just experienced will be repeated again."

"Oh. I don't know that I could handle another explosion such as that one again." She truly did look alarmed.

"Hold on, sweetheart. You go right ahead and enjoy yourself. I am here to catch you when you fly."

***

I am here to catch you when you fly.

That was precisely how she'd felt when that wonderful, marvelous feeling swept over her, like she was soaring through the clouds, way above earth, looking down on the mere mortals who were not there with her. Had she ever known how exciting a man and a woman joining together was, she would not have waited this long to experience it.

Except she'd never met another man with whom she wanted to share such an intimacy.

Until she'd met Simon.

She was not sure what that meant, but did not plan to dwell on it while he was moving inside her and the feelings from before were building once again. "Oh, that feels wonderful, too. Does it feel good for you, too?"

"Yes. It certainly does."

"How does it feel for you?"

"Good lord, woman, you want to hold an intellectual discussion now? If so, I'm afraid I must decline since I am hardly dressed for the part."

They both laughed, and Simon looked strangely at her, as if pleasantly surprised. Taking the opportunity, she pulled his head down and kissed him; this time she nudged his lips and he opened. She used her tongue to taste the inside of his mouth, sweeping in, taking all he offered. Brandy, something sweet, something minty. And most of all, Simon.

The fullness inside her felt strange at first, then as he began a steady rhythm the feelings from before began to build again. She released his lips on a sigh. He tucked his head against her neck and murmured in her ear as he continued to move. "I've wanted you for so long. You can't possibly know how good it feels to be inside you, to feel your heated softness surrounding me."

As his actions continued, her excitement rose once again and she felt the build-up in her lower parts that would lead to another explosion. Or as Simon had said, send her flying. She clung to his shoulders, straining, her muscles tense, all of her focused on where they were joined. She moved her hips and he groaned, "Yes, do that."

He cupped her head and smothered her lips with demanding mastery. Simon shifted slightly and reached between them. She sucked in a breath when his finger rubbed against a part of her that immediately brought her the waves of pleasure she'd had before. Simon gave one final thrust and groaned her name. She felt the rush of his seed as it entered her.

It was then that she realized there could very well be consequences from their actions. She pushed the idea aside since she knew from all her reading that it would be quite rare for conception to take place from one act. And, after what she'd experienced, she had no intention for this to be their only time.

She played with his hair as their breathing returned to normal. "Simon?"

"Um," he panted out his answer, then rolled off her, pulling her next to his body.

"Aren't there methods a man can use to avoid conception?"

He rose up on his elbow and stared at her. "I believe it is a little too late to ask that. I'm afraid the deed has been done. And now I realize how foolish I have been to not consider that beforehand."

She waved her hand. "I know. But conception is not likely the very first time." At his surprised expression, she said. "I am well-read, you know. I was wondering for the future."

"The future?"

"Yes." She sat up, and much to Simon's amusement, given his expression, she wiggled her bottom until she rested against the headboard. Seeing his hungry look at her breasts, she pulled the sheet up to her neck. "I told you I wanted us to be lovers. I'm assuming since you're here, that you agree?"

He joined her at the headboard and took her hand in his, intertwining their fingers. "Elise. Gently reared unmarried women do not take lovers."

She shifted so she could look at him. "And?"

"And you are a gently reared unmarried woman."

With raised eyebrows, she said, "Was I a gently reared unmarried woman when you entered my bedroom tonight?" Why was he being so peculiar? He looked almost guilty. Or something strange.

"Yes, of course you were."

"And did you leave when you remembered I was a gently reared unmarried woman?"

He sighed and rolled his eyes. "I told you when I arrived that I didn't think it was a good idea."

She tapped her chin with her index finger. "Again. Did that cause you to leave?"

"Of course not." He waved his hand at their bodies. "I believe that is obvious."

Elise raised her chin and regarded him. "Are you telling me this is a one-time event?"

"Uh, no." He ran his fingers through his hair and dropped his head back to stare at the bed canopy. He turned to her and at her all-knowing smirk, he added, "I mean . . ."

"What do you mean?"

He hesitated for almost a full minute, then said, "I think we should get married."

CHAPTER SEVEN

Elise turned to him, her mouth agape. "Married!" He was afraid after all their activities not drawing any attention, her outburst would be the one that would have her family—particularly her father—pounding on the door. Of course what her father would demand was precisely what he'd just suggested.

"Yes. You know, that ceremony performed in front of witnesses where one pledges his troth to another?" Somehow it didn't appear that Elise found his flippant remarks humorous. "Why not?"

"Not only do I not believe you just said *I think we should get married*, but I'm finding it hard to understand why you think I should agree with you."

"I think we would rub along quite well." In fact, even though he'd blurted it out, the more he thought about it, the better the idea seemed to be. He would undoubtedly enjoy climbing into bed every night with Elise. She certainly showed a great deal of enthusiasm and adventure. And even though he had his brother and nephew to inherit, maybe he could have a son of his own.

The thought was warming. He could have a son whom he would never abandon, either from running away or by killing himself.

"How very *ton* of you," she sniffed.

He frowned. "What does that mean?"

"*Rubbing along together* is no reason for us to get married."

"Well, maybe the fact that we we're sitting in your bed naked as the day we were born might be."

"I thought we agreed we would be lovers. Have an affair?"

"I never agreed to that."

"Well, you're sitting here, aren't you?

"This isn't an affair."

"What is it?"

Simon took a deep breath. This was getting them nowhere. He had to make Elise understand that they could not have an affair and she maintain her reputation. No matter how hard one tried, those things were always discovered and word would spread like a wild fire.

He took her hand, which she reluctantly allowed. "It is my duty and responsibility to marry you after what happened." What the devil was wrong now? She stiffened like a board and the look she cast him would scare the devil himself. "What?"

"I do not want to be anyone's responsibility or duty. I want to be a free woman, who makes my own decisions and suffers whatever consequences, myself."

Losing his patience with the way the conversation was going, he jumped from the bed and tugged on his breeches. When he noticed the look on her face as she regarded him, he almost pulled them off and climbed back into bed with her. That would never do. They had to get this settled.

"Even if we managed to avoid discovery—which, given the gossips in the *ton* seems impossible to me—there is always the chance of creating a child—"

He held up his hand as Elise opened her mouth to speak. "The methods available are not foolproof. There is more than one child in the *ton* carrying the name of a man other than his true father."

Elise shook her head. "We appear to be at a standstill. I never intended to marry and, as you know, we began this relationship so you would keep me from having to deal with men who might be interested in marriage."

"I agree that it appears we are at a standstill, my dear. I will not continue in an affair. You have no idea what you are asking. I would be labeled a cad and a dishonorable man, and you would be branded every sort of horrible name that would disgrace you and your family." He dropped his shirt over his head and tucked it into his breeches. "If you do not care for your own reputation, think of your sisters."

Elise rose to her knees, still clutching the sheet to her neck. Her hair tumbled around her in tangles, her cheeks were flushed, and her lips swollen. The entire back area of her body was visible and he had to tamp down the groan about to escape.

"How dare you bring my sisters into this? I adore my sisters and would do anything for them."

Simon shrugged into his jacket. "Except marry."

She slumped. That took the wind out of her sails. "That was unkind."

He placed his hands on his hips. "But true."

"So you won't change your mind?" She raised her chin.

"Will you change yours?" Since he had taken to the idea of marriage, he had this obsession to have her agree. He had decided to never marry, but now he was just as adamant that he would marry. And it would be to no one else except Lady Elise Smith.

She skirted his question. "Be careful leaving. Papa sometimes goes to the kitchen for warm milk."

He walked to her and kissed her on the forehead. "Good night."

Luckily, everything was quiet as he made his way down the corridor to the back staircase. He let himself out of the house through the—thankfully empty—kitchen. He headed to the mews and retrieved Diamond, vaulting onto his back and turning the reins to walk the animal out of the stable and to the street.

He stopped in front of the Pomeroy townhouse and stared up at Elise's window. All was dark. She'd blown out the candles. Turning his horse toward the end of the street he continued on to his house, thinking of the significant decision he'd made.

Elise did not want a husband because she worried about losing her independence. He would give her as much of a free hand as he could. She was being foolish. Did she think her father had forgotten about Blackwell? If she refused Simon, Blackwell was her future.

He shook his head. An affair. That was as likely to remain a secret as a race through Mayfair at four o'clock in the afternoon. Admittedly he could have done a better job of proposing marriage, but being the sensible women she was, he assumed she would see the wisdom of his idea without the romantic nonsense.

He thought back to their lovemaking. Yes, he'd wanted her, almost from the time they met, but now having had her, he wanted her more than ever. He would have her, too. But on his terms, not hers. This was a war, and he would be the victor. And to the victor belonged the spoils. In this case, a fiery, stubborn, intelligent, and adventurous woman.

Be aware, Lady Elise. The battle has just begun.

***

Elise stared at the closed door Simon just left through.

Married!

Whatever made him say that? Of course she was no dimwit and knew once a gently reared unmarried woman lost her virtue, marriage was the typical *ton* response. But there were generally two reasons for that. One, they were caught, and two, one's future husband would wonder about her missing hymen.

They had not been caught and, since she had no intention of ever marrying, there was no husband in her future who would be searching for the missing body part on their wedding night. She slapped the covers. Oh, the man was impossible! He had taken something truly wonderful and decided to withhold it from her until she complied with his wishes. That was precisely why she'd eschewed marriage. Everything always had to be the man's way. They held all the power. Or, in this case, the necessary equipment. Despite her annoyance, that brought a giggle.

She jumped from the bed and slipped into her nightgown. It was then she noticed the slight bit of blood on her sheet. That would never do. She quickly drew on her dressing gown and hurried downstairs to the linen closet and retrieved a fresh sheet. Once the bed linen was changed—certainly not like the maid would have done it—she glanced around her room, holding the soiled sheet, wondering what to do with it. Maybe she should hang it out the window like the Scottish lairds had in the past. She snorted at that idea, thinking that would be a sure way to bring notice to her fall from virtue.

She shoved it under the bed for now and crawled under the covers, lying on her back. What would marriage to Simon be like? She gave herself time to consider it. He was handsome, titled, rich, and knew what to do in bed. They were certainly excellent recommendations. He was also smart, considerate, and had a sense of humor that matched her own. She could certainly do worse.

She flopped over onto her stomach. One time, when she was a young girl and assumed, like everyone else, she would one day marry her Prince Charming, she'd decided she would only marry for love. Then, somewhere along the line she'd become disenchanted with the gentlemen of the *ton,* found them silly and groping. At the same time she discovered she was very happy with her little circle of scholarly friends. And her independence.

It had been then that she'd determined to remain single and enjoy her freedom. No husband to answer to, or ask permission from, or bow to his wishes.

No love. No children.

But why was she battering herself? Simon's attempt at a proposal—as pathetic and overbearing as it had been—never mentioned love, or caring, or affection, or anything along those lines. All he spoke of was duty and responsibility. Could she love him?

Scary thought, that. She had to admit there was a great deal about him to encourage love. His sense of humor, his caring, the way he had held his own with her friends at her gathering, and, most of all, how he looked at her that had her heart pounding and her insides melting.

After their lovemaking, she would be fooling herself to not acknowledge her feelings toward him had changed. Most likely intimacy with a man did that. They had been naked together, with nothing between them, nowhere to hide. More than their bodies had been uncovered, their raw emotions had been exposed to each other, brought into the light. Never had she opened herself up like that before. Not even with her sisters. It truly had been a life-altering experience. With a deep sigh at all these heavy thoughts, she closed her eyes and ordered herself to sleep.

Her body did not obey the order for hours.

The next morning, she entered the breakfast room to join her sisters and Papa. "Good morning, everyone."

Papa lowered his newspaper and gave her a brilliant smile. "Good morning, daughter."

Juliet and Marigold wished her good day, and Elise made her way to the sideboard to fill her breakfast plate with egg, bacon, creamed trout, and bread warm from the oven. Apparently bed activities had given her an appetite.

She'd been a bit sore when she awoke that morning, which should not have been a surprise. But once the memories of the night before had washed over her, she again grew irritated at Simon for refusing to have an affair and demanding marriage instead.

"Elise, once you finish your breakfast, I would speak with you in my study."

"Yes, Papa." Good lord, had he seen Simon leaving the night before? No. He would not look so placid had he witnessed her lover creeping down the stairs and out the back door.

Her lover.

She blushed, loving that phrase.

"Are you well, Elise?" Juliet eyed her with concern.

"Yes. Why do you ask?"

"You seemed a bit stiff when you walked into the room and just now your face flushed quite red."

Elise waved her off. "I am fine. It is a tad warm in here." As if to reinforce her subterfuge she waved her napkin in her face. Both Juliet and Marigold viewed her with suspicion. Papa ignored her. Blast her sisters who never missed anything.

Papa rose and bowed to them. "Have a pleasant day, my loves. I await your presence, Elise."

"Yes, Papa."

Once she finished her breakfast, Elise joined her father in his study. He was bent over a stack of correspondence, looking every inch the nobleman. Even in the confines of his home, he wore a starched cravat, waistcoat, and jacket over his buff breeches.

Remembering last night, the thought popped into her head that Papa probably had the same desires as other men. Was he having an affair?

Lord, she pushed that image out of her head in a hurry.

"Papa, you wanted to speak with me?"

He sat back, admiring her. "Yes, my dear. How lovely you look today."

"Thank you." She took a seat in front of his desk.

As was his habit, he rose and strolled around the desk, resting his hip on the edge, swinging his foot. "I have good news for you."

She viewed him with raised eyebrows. "What, Papa?"

"We are getting close to signing marriage contract papers with Lord Blackwell." He beamed at her as if he'd just offered her the greatest of gifts.

***

Simon jumped from his horse and left the animal with the stable master at the mews behind Elise's townhouse. He'd learned that tonight she was holding another of her intellectual gatherings. It had been five days since he'd left her bedroom.

Five long days. Followed by five long nights. He missed her terribly. She was constantly on his mind. So many times he wanted to give in and agree to an affair, just to have her in his arms again. But then he pulled back. He wanted her for always, for his wife, for the mother of his children. If he were to give in once, he would never be able to hold firm to his decision for them to wed.

He'd purposely stayed away from the *ton* events he thought she would be attending, and eschewed rides in the park so as not to run into her. However, once he discovered her gathering this evening, he could not stay away. But at least with other people in such a small setting, he would be refrained from dragging her into another room and having his way with her.

The man at the door nodded and directed him to the drawing room from where voices rose. It took him only a second to spot Elise. She stood speaking with a group of guests, but her usual sparkle was missing. She seemed to be doing more nodding than arm waving and speaking. A man in her group noticed him and said something to Elise.

She turned and he caught his breath. She looked terrible.

She was pale, and he swore she'd lost weight in the five days since he'd seen her last. Her eyes grew wide and she hurried over to him. "I need to speak with you."

"I am here."

"No. In private. Something has happened, and I need your help. I tried to send a note, but there was no one I trusted not to tell Papa."

"Where can we go?"

She shook her head. "Not now. It must be after everyone leaves."

He took her ice-cold hand. "Calm down, Elise. All will be well. Whatever it is, we can take care of it together."

Nodding briskly, she took his arm and walked him to the group she had just left. Why everyone else didn't notice her unease surprised him. Or perhaps he knew her so well? He attempted to focus on the conversation, but he was so taken with Elise's demeanor that not much of what he heard made sense.

It was way too soon for her to know if she was with child. What else could possibly have her in this state? Besides her cold fingers, she tended to lose track of what she was saying. She picked at her gown and kept shifting her feet. A scatter-brained Elise was quite surprising. Eventually the footmen arrived with a light repast that Elise did not eat, but she drank three cups of tea. Had he access to brandy, he would have dropped a bit into her cup.

Once the last guest had departed, she took his hand and dragged him into the library, closing the door. "I am in big trouble."

His first thought was her father had discovered what they'd done, but then realized the man would have been at his front door with a pistol had that been the case. "What is it?"

Elise began to pace, wringing her hands. "Papa told me the day after we—" She stopped and took a deep breath.

"Go on."

"Yes. Anyway, that very next morning he called me into his study to tell me he and Lord Blackwell were close to signing marriage papers."

Simon felt as though his entire world had just been yanked out from under him. Marriage contracts? He stared at her, his thoughts numb.

After the shock wore off, anger tightened his stomach muscles. Elise was his. He'd already claimed her. "You can't marry Blackwell. You're going to marry me."

She threw her hands up. "No one listens. I am not going to marry anyone."

He placed his hands on her shoulders. "Hear me, Elise. It appears you have two choices. Either marry Blackwell or marry me. Since you are no longer a virgin, the decision is already made."

She yanked herself away from his grip. "No. The decision has not been made."

Simon pointed to a chair near the fireplace. "Sit."

Elise opened her mouth to object, but something

in his face must have changed her mind, and she took the seat. He strode across the room and poured them both a brandy. He handed one to her. "Drink."

"I am not a dog, you know." She downed the brandy, then spent a full minute coughing and wiping watery eyes.

Simon sat alongside her. "Do you want to marry Blackwell?"

"No. But I have an idea."

He cringed. Elise's ideas were not always the most thought out. "What?"

"Why don't you approach Papa and tell him you are considering making me an offer. Then he will hold off Blackwell until the end of the Season. By then Blackwell will probably lose interest."

Simon stared at her for a minute, not believing what he'd just heard. "Let me get this straight. You want me to tell your father that I am considering making an offer for you, when I have, in fact, already proposed to you and you refused. Then we will all act as though everything is perfectly normal and this will keep Blackwell away?"

She nodded, apparently quite pleased with herself. "Yes."

He dragged her into his arms and did what he'd been obsessed with the past five days. His lips covered hers, demanding, taking, possessing. Her enthusiasm, no longer so innocent, sent his senses reeling. Had he locked the door when they'd entered, he would strip her down and have a repeat performance of their last time together.

Their hands were everywhere, but soon he realized that the door was not locked, and, as much as he'd like to be caught with her in his arms, that most likely would not go well with Elise. He drew back, both of them panting.

"You must find another solution, sweetheart. If I ask your father to consider an offer from me, it will be real, not a ruse. I'm finished with pretending."

Pulling himself together, he stood and straightened his jacket. Bending down, he kissed the top of her head and left the house. The fresh air felt good on his heated skin. What a conundrum this had become. Nevertheless, of one thing he was certain.

Lady Elise Smith would marry no one but him.

CHAPTER EIGHT

Elise twirled around the dance floor with Lord Blackwell. Her hands were damp under her gloves, and her stomach tightened with nerves. She had decided to do what had to be done to discourage the man. Once he and her father signed marriage contracts she would be doomed. Truth be known, if her plan did not work and she were forced to marry anyone, it would be Simon.

Of course, he would have to do a much better job of proposing. Duty and responsibility, indeed! No woman wanted to someone's penance. If she could get out of marriage altogether, that would be perfect. Unless Simon was truly her knight in shining armor and found it in his heart to offer a proposal that would literally sweep her off her feet.

The music came to an end and Elise took a deep breath. "My lord, would you be so kind as to escort me to the gardens? There is a matter I wish to discuss with you."

"Of course." He took her elbow and wended their way through the crowd to the French doors leading to the patio.

Once they were outside, she took his arm and they stepped onto the path surrounding the flowers. They'd walked for about five minutes when Elise pulled Blackwell toward a stone bench under an oak tree.

Once seated, she turned to him, twisting her hands in her lap. "I am most sorry to have to say this, but I cannot marry you, my lord."

His eyebrows rose in a quizzical twist, and she continued. "Papa told me you were in the process of negotiating marriage contracts."

"Is that what he told you?" Lord, Blackwell actually seemed surprised. Was he so old that his memory was fading?

"Yes. I know he probably should have not said anything to me until you spoke with me first, but he did, and now I must tell you." She stopped and took a deep breath. "I cannot marry you. I am so sorry."

Blackwell almost looked as if he was holding in laughter. Did he not take her seriously? She raised her chin. "There is a very serious reason why I cannot marry you."

He rearranged his face into a more sober mien. "And what is that?"

Chewing on her lip, she blurted, "I am no longer untouched."

"Excuse me?"

"I am not a maiden."

He continued to stare at her. Was the man not familiar with the words she was using? How else could she state it that he would understand she could not marry him? Heat rose to her face at having to elaborate on the subject. "My lord, what I am trying to say—"

Blackwell held his hand up. "I, um. You don't need to elaborate, I think I know what you mean."

"Good." She breathed a sigh of relief, which

quickly grew into panic when he stood, his hands fisted at his side, his face twisted in anger. "Where is he?"

"Who?" Maybe if she pretended not to know who he was talking about they could return to the ballroom and have this extremely uncomfortable conversation over with.

"St. George. I am not blind, Lady Elise. I intend to call him out and then advise your father of this disaster."

"Call him out? Advise Papa? Disaster? Oh, no, no, please. You mustn't make a matter of contention out of this."

"Lady Elise, you have been compromised. St. George must be brought up to scratch."

She placed her hand on his chest. "No. No. He already has."

He looked down at her, confusion clearly written on his face. "He has, what?"

"He has *ordered* me to marry him!"

Again Blackwell looked as though he would laugh. He was certainly a strange man. Not once had he railed against losing her because of her "condition." He seemed more outraged on her behalf than at him being thwarted.

"My dear, you must marry him."

She pushed aside the urge to stamp her foot like a child. "I will not be told that I must marry." They stood staring at each other, then Elise remembered one other point. "Oh, my lord, I also must ask a favor of you."

He ran his fingers through his hair. It amazed her how many men had that habit. "What is that?"

She primly entwined her fingers at her waist and

smiled up at him. "When you visit with my father to withdraw your offer, you must not tell him why." If Papa found out about Simon, he would demand a wedding. And somehow she was sure his demand would involve a pistol.

"I don't think I can agree to that." He shook his head. "This is serious business and you must let your father handle this with St. George."

"Please?" She continued to stare at him, and the tears that filled her eyes were genuine. She wanted time to think about her and Simon. Being rushed into marriage, never knowing his feelings, or for that matter, her own, could plague her the rest of her life.

He blew out a deep breath. "This is not a good idea." He looked beyond her shoulder for a moment, staring into the darkened garden. "Very well. However, I cannot be held to that promise if it appears to me that confiding in your father—with his promise not to act in haste—would be in your best interests." With that nebulous answer that she ruminated in her mind, he extended his arm to her. "Now I think we should return to the ballroom before tongues begin to wag."

They walked slowly back, which gave Elise time to compose herself. She felt better knowing she wouldn't be compelled to marry Blackwell while she was still trying to come to grips with her relationship with Simon.

"What is the meaning of this?" Thinking of Simon conjured up the man, blocking their path, legs braced apart, his arms crossed over his chest.

Blackwell removed her arm from his. "What is that supposed to mean, St. George?"

"What it means is why are you and Lady Elise

out here in a dark garden?"

Lord Blackwell leaned forward. "And why is that your affair?"

"It is my affair because Lady Elise is no longer available. She will shortly be betrothed."

"Who has approved that?" Elise chimed in.

"I have," he snapped.

Blackwell moved away from Elise. "Before this goes any further, there is something I need to do."

Simon frowned. "What?"

"This." Blackwell drew his arm back and punched Simon smack on the jaw.

Tugging on the cuffs of his jacket, he turned on his heel and headed toward the ballroom. When he got to the door, he turned. "I will leave Lady Elise in your hands, but I will expect to see the two of you back in the ballroom directly."

***

Dazed, Simon sat on the stone pathway, holding his face. It did not require too much brain power to know Elise had told the man of their indiscretion. He waved away her arm when she bent to help him up. "I can get up myself."

Rising, he brushed off his breeches and straightened his jacket. "Am I to assume you told Blackwell? I can't think of any other reason for the man to hit me."

"Yes."

Holding his chin, he worked his jaw. The pain wasn't too bad. He had a feeling the man didn't come at him full throttle. "You do realize he will go directly to your father with this news?"

Elise shook her head. "No. I made him promise he wouldn't tell Papa why I could not marry him."

"And he promised?"

"Well, sort of."

Raised eyebrows had her squirming. "He seemed to promise. The way he worded it, I am not too sure, but as a gentleman, I am sure he will keep his word."

"Whatever that word was. You don't seem to be too clear on that point." Simon placed his hands on his hips. "May I ask what your purpose was in involving Lord Blackwell in something that should have remained between us?"

This entire conversation was becoming more uncomfortable by the minute. "Since you refused to go along with my plan for you to speak to Papa on my behalf to remove Lord Blackwell from contention, I had to take matters into my own hands."

"And you felt this was the best solution to your dilemma? The idea that once Blackwell found out you were not a woman of virtue, he would withdraw his suit?"

"Exactly." She beamed if she'd finally gotten through to him.

Simon shook his head. "Let us return to the ballroom. We have been out here much too long. I do not wish to have Blackwell come at me again, because this time I will be prepared." As he took her elbow, he said, "I thought Lady Dearborn was your chaperone. I haven't seen her in weeks."

"No. That was for that one evening. Actually Papa is our chaperone."

He stared at her. "I saw him in the card room not ten minutes ago."

"I am sure he doesn't feel I need a chaperone at my great age."

He snorted. "My dear, if anyone needs a

chaperone, it is you."

Despite the agony it caused him, Simon stayed away from Elise the next week. If Blackwell had told Pomeroy about him and Elise, there was no doubt in his mind he would have had a visit from her father. Most likely accompanied by the parson.

He'd had himself convinced he should forget the whole mess and go back to his original plan of never marrying and letting his brother assume his title when the time came. Then he would think about Elise laughing as they waltzed, whacking her ball with fervor at the Townsend garden party, and writhing with passion underneath him. His world would never be the same without her in it.

Bloody hell, was he to repeat his father's actions and grow despondent over a woman? That frightened him enough to ring for his valet to prepare a bath and dress him for the Stevenson ball. He had no idea if Elise would be present, but it was time to put it all behind him and resume his normal routine of attending society events and playing cat-and-mouse with the mamas of the *ton,* as he'd done for years.

Feeling almost himself, he handed his invitation to the butler at the top of the stairs and waited to be announced. No, he would not scan the crowd for Lady Elise Smith. Instead, he descended the stairs and found a congenial group of men who discussed politics and horses. Soon, he was surrounded by other friends and ladies anxious for his attention.

He tried to believe that life had returned to normal. He added his name to a number of dance cards and held more conversations with a few lords about the latest goings-on in parliament. But no matter how hard he tried, the entire time he felt as though he were missing part of himself. No woman made him burst out with laughter or tempted him to pull her closer when they waltzed. The champagne lay flat on his tongue and the discussions leaned toward the boring.

Deciding a trip to the card room might be a pleasant distraction, he excused himself from Lord Alway and Miss Benton as they chatted about the latest *on dit* and headed in that direction. He made his way through the crowd and entered the card room.

Lord Pomeroy sat with three other men, one of whom, Mr. Butler, rose from his seat and left the room. Quickly, before another man took the seat, Simon pulled out the chair and sat. "Good evening, gentlemen."

They all nodded, except Pomeroy who studied him. "Haven't seen you in a while, St. George. I thought you left town."

"No, sir. I have been busy."

"Is that right?" He began dealing the cards and then took a sip of his drink before he picked up his hand. "Lady Elise has one of those infernal gatherings coming up this week."

Simon tried to concentrate on the game, but he wasn't sure exactly what it was Pomeroy was trying to tell him. If all had gone as Elise had planned, Blackwell would have withdrawn his suit by now. Since Simon was no longer hanging about, perhaps Elise would get her wish and her father would cease in his scheme to get her married off.

Why did that thought bother him? Hadn't he decided just tonight to resume his normal life and forget about the distracting woman?

Is that so? Then how come I am sitting at her father's table?

They continued their play. "Crafty young lady, my girl."

Was there an answer to that? Was that even a question? Not quite sure, Simon grunted and sipped his drink.

He threw coins into the pile in the center of the table and tried very hard to concentrate on his hand. He'd never played so badly, even to the point where Mr. Aldridge looked over at him with a quizzical expression at his last play.

"I've been thinking about a dinner party."

All three men turned to Pomeroy and studied him. He ignored them and continued to play his hand as though he'd never spoken. Aldridge looked at Simon with raised eyebrows. Simon shrugged.

Play continued.

"Maybe Thursday, next."

Now the other men ignored *him*. Pomeroy turned to Simon. "Lady Elise loves to ride her horse first thing in the morning. Refuses to take a groom with her." He shook his head.

Simon signaled a footman to bring him another brandy. He gulped it down and set the glass aside. He was tempted to ask for a refill, but his playing was bad enough with the distraction of Pomeroy uttering random thoughts. Perhaps the man intended to coerce Simon into losing enough money that he would need for Elise's "very nice" dowry.

After two more rounds, Pomeroy threw down his hand and stood. "I believe I will gather my two younger daughters." He turned to Simon. "My eldest is home with a megrim. Then I am headed for home." He bowed and said, "Gentlemen, it's been a pleasure."

With three sets of curious eyes on him, Pomeroy left the card room, whistling softly as he made his way out the door.

***

Lord Pomeroy sat in his study, staring off into space, thinking about his lovely eldest daughter. The light of his life and currently the bane of his existence. Still determined to get her married, and soon, he went over his plan in his mind. The idea of having her marry before accepting offers for her sisters was brilliant.

Had he not tied her sisters' happiness to Elise marrying, she would have lingered in his home for the remainder of his days. Not that he objected to the girl's presence. She was truly a wonderful household manager, of a most congenial nature, and a fine mother to his younger girls. Even though he'd believed his motivation had been to lessen the daily arrival of bills, truth be known, once he'd seen her and St. George together, he knew Elise deserved the true love he'd had with his deceased wife. He wanted that for all his girls.

Even the reluctant one.

For some unknown reason, things were at a standstill. St. George no longer called, and Elise spent too much time in her bedchamber. Telling her that he and Blackwell were close to signing marriage contracts had frightened her at first, but soon after she seemed accepting of her fate, which was not the Elise he knew.

There had been several empty chairs at the card

tables last night when St. George had entered the room, but he specifically took the one Butler had given up. So the young man was not avoiding him. Which led him to believe whatever happened between Elise and her young man was not on St. George's side.

"My lord, Lord Blackwell requests an audience." His butler, Mason, stood at the doorway, stiff and proper as always.

"Yes. Send him in, my good man." Maybe Blackwell had some insight as to what was going on.

Pomeroy rose and greeted Blackwell, waving to the chairs in front of the fireplace. "Mason, please have Cook send in coffee and pastries."

Mason bowed and left the room.

They spoke of banal things until the refreshments had been placed in front of them and each man had fixed his coffee to his liking. Pomeroy took a sip and placed the cup on the saucer. "To what do I owe the honor of this visit, Blackwell?"

Blackwell leaned back and rested his booted foot on his knee. "I have been aware of a situation for some time now and decided the moment had arrived for me to share it with you."

"All right. I admit you have my interest piqued."

"This is about Lady Elise."

Pomeroy nodded for the man to continue. He looked rather serious, and Pomeroy wondered if there was something he needed to be concerned about. When it came to his girls he was indeed the papa who righted wrongs and solved problems. If St. George had hurt her delicate heart, he would pay.

"Almost two weeks ago at one of the balls — I don't remember which one, since after a while they all tend to run together — Lady Elise requested I escort her on a stroll around the garden. She seemed a bit unsettled and said there was something she needed to discuss with me." Blackwell took another sip of coffee, then pushed the cup away. "Lady Elise told me she could not marry me."

Pomeroy grinned. Leave it to his darling little girl to address an issue with direct confrontation. "Indeed? And what did you say?"

"Obviously, I was taken aback by her direct words. Then I realized since it was Lady Elise, she would never be the wilting flower, wringing-of-hands type. In fact, I had to hide my smile at her directness."

"Go on."

"This is where it gets rather sticky, and I need you to keep a cool head about you."

Pomeroy's stomach muscles tightened at Blackwell's words, but he waved his hand for the man to continue. Whatever had Elise gotten herself into now? As much as he loved the girl, he was certain the few silver strands on his head had come courtesy of his eldest.

"It seems she and St. George have been intimate, and she wanted to let me know that since I would no doubt expect a pure bride, it would not be her."

All the blood drained from Pomeroy's head, then raced back up to set his heart pounding. He felt as though it would explode. He hopped up from his seat, his hands fisted at his side.

"Whoa, Pomeroy, calm down."

He grabbed Blackwell by his cravat. "And you are only telling me this now?" He would find St. George and shoot him dead, then drag his corpse to the altar. His little girl was an innocent and no doubt the lecher had seduced and ruined her.

Wide-eyed, Blackwell stared at him, his face growing red as Pomeroy continued to squeeze his cravat. Seeing his friend's distress, Pomeroy growled, then released him, and sat back down. Blackwell adjusted his cravat and took a deep breath. "There is more."

His fingers gripped the arms of the chair and he glared at his guest. "Continue."

"When I told her you needed to know because St. George had to be brought up to scratch, she calmly informed me the man had *ordered her*—her words—to marry him and she refused."

Pomeroy dropped his head into his hands. Why the devil hadn't he produced sons? A son he could take to Gentlemen Jackson's and beat the living hell out of him. Or toss him to the wolves, or any number of things that would rid him of problems. But daughters? One raised voice and they dissolved into tears, and he was left feeling like the biggest ogre in London.

"One other thing."

His head jerked up. "There's more?" God don't let the gel be with child.

"She made me promise I would not tell you why I was withdrawing my offer of marriage. I told her I would not break her confidence unless I thought it was in her best interests if you knew. Since I have reason to believe the two of them are at odds with each other at present, I felt it was time to come to you with this knowledge."

Pomeroy slumped in his chair for a few minutes, staring into space.

"What will you do?" Blackwell asked.

"Pour myself a bloody large glass of brandy. Then pay a visit to the Viscount St. George."

CHAPTER NINE

Elise bent over and used her finger to check herself one more time, then groaned. Nothing. Her courses still had not started. It had been three weeks since Simon had made love to her right here in this very room when she had so blithely informed him that, being as well read as she was, there was almost no chance one coupling would produce a child.

Fool, her.

What would she do now? Well, for one thing, she would have to find the calm, cool Elise deep inside her who always handled any issue with aplomb and grace. Moaning aloud, she sank to her knees and pounded on the carpet. "What will I do?" she shouted to the walls.

"Elise?" Juliet stood in her doorway, obviously having just risen from her bed, a puzzled look on her face. "Are you all right?"

Well, then. So much for being calm and collected. It was a wonder she hadn't roused the entire household. She gave her sister a smile and pushed the hair out of her face. "Yes, I am fine."

"Why are you on your knees?"

"I dropped a coin and was searching for it under the bed."

Juliet looked from where Elise knelt on the carpet to where the bed stood halfway across the room. She closed the door behind her, walked to Elise, and sat cross-legged on the floor next to her. "What is wrong?"

Elise shifted and drew up her legs and wrapped her arms around them, resting her chin on her knees. "Nothing."

Juliet smirked. "Not true," she said in a sing-song voice that always irritated Elise. "Something is the matter with you. You were thrashing about in your bed last night, and I came to your room. You were mumbling something about 'Simon.' Isn't that St. George's Christian name?"

"Yes." Elise sighed. "That is his name."

Juliet shifted until she was in the same position as Elise. "Marigold and I thought things were going quite well with St. George."

Elise shrugged.

"I saw you dancing with Mr. Howard at the Folger ball the other evening. He seems like a nice sort. Not bad to look at. And rich, I understand."

"And only interested in his hounds and horses." Elise stood and moved to the dressing table and sat, then picked up her brush. "Besides, I don't want a husband."

Juliet moved behind her and took the brush from her hand and began to run it through Elise's long hair. "Do you think Papa will really refuse offers for me and Marigold next Season if you do not marry?"

"I had a plan that I hoped would dissuade him from that edict."

Her sister's raised eyebrows questioned her.

"Lord St. George and I struck a bargain. He would pretend to court me to keep other men away, then at the end of the Season he would return to his normal life and I would tell Papa that I am unmarriageable, in which case he would admit his mistake, and all would be well."

Juliet stared at her in the mirror. All of a sudden, her face lit up. "You've fallen in love with him!"

Elise spun around, knocking the brush from her sister's hand. "What? No. No. Of course not." The tingle that began in her stomach turned into a hot flush that rose to her face until she felt as though she was on fire.

Love? Surely not.

Juliet grinned. "Of course you have."

In love with Simon? No, never. She shook her head, picked up the brush from the floor and returned it to the dressing table. Leaning forward, she studied herself in the mirror. What did love look like? Feel like? So far all she suffered from were symptoms of an ague. Warm skin, upset stomach, restlessness, a headache, overwhelming fatigue.

Or breeding.

Dear God, please don't make that be the cause. She'd rather be in love. She wanted more than anything to talk to Simon, tell him about her fears. He would be able to calm her, make her see reason. He was good at that.

Nonsense. If he thought for one second that she was increasing, he would escort her to her father and between the two of them she would be standing in front of the vicar before she had time to change her shoes.

"If you are in love with St. George, and it seems obvious to me, why are the two of you no longer courting?" Juliet's jaw dropped. "Oh, Elise! Did he toss you over? It's that horrid Miss Abbott, isn't it?"

"No. He didn't toss me over." She chewed her lip. "He wants to marry me."

All the air seemed to leave Juliet's lungs, and she backed up until she sat on the edge of the bed. "Marry you?"

Elise nodded. "Yes."

"Isn't that good news? I mean, I know you never wanted to marry, but Papa is insisting on it, you are in love with St. George—don't scowl at me because you know you are—and he wants to marry you."

"Two reasons." Elise stood and paced back and forth, much like she had the night she waited for Simon in this very room. Considering the consequences that might result from said evening, she pushed it from her mind.

"One." She raised a finger. "I am terrified of being married. I know it sounds foolish to you since it has been your heart's desire since you were a little girl, but I have known freedom and independence like few women of the *ton* enjoy. Except for wealthy widows, of course." She stopped and regarded her sister. "As a married woman, I would have to gain permission to do the things I do every day without thought.

"Also, viscountesses are expected to hold dinner parties, soirees, balls, garden parties, and those sorts of events. I have never wanted to be part of that, nor would I be good at it. I like my intellectual gatherings."

"Didn't his lordship attend a couple of your gatherings?"

Elise nodded.

"There, you see. He appreciates your interests, especially if he came back a second time."

"How do I know he would continue to approve of my gatherings? Perhaps it was all a ruse." The memory of him taking a genuine interest in the conversations going on around him disputed her words. He had not been pretending; he had seemed truly intrigued by her friends.

"Elise, dearest, I have been to one of your gatherings. Anyone who comes back for a return visit was not feigning anything."

"I believe you have just insulted me."

Juliet hopped up and wrapped her arms around her sister. "You know I love you, and approve of anything you do, but your events are just not to my taste." She smiled. "Forgive me?"

Elise patted her hand. "Of course. I know what

we discuss does not appeal to everyone."

"All right, so we've covered the supposed change in your lifestyle that marriage would force upon you, and it seems that is not likely. What is your second reason?"

"Wait, we're not finished with my independence. I would not care to ask permission to do anything I wish to do. Papa has never questioned me or tried to curb my activities." Years of being able to do as she pleased without accounting to anyone made for a wonderful life, and not one she wanted to change.

"Until now," Juliet said.

"True. But a husband would be much worse."

"How so?" Juliet paused and laughed. "Don't look at me that way. I am serious. You are also forgetting the good things about marriage."

Like being able to enjoy bed activities with Simon.

She ticked off on her fingers. "You will run your own house."

"I do now."

Juliet shook her head. "No. It's Papa's house. Also, you will have children to love and teach." She took Elise's hand. "You would be a wonderful mother. You have always been one to me and Marigold."

"True." Her stomach twisted at her sister's words since they may have already started on that project.

"What is your second reason?"

"Although I say he wants to marry me, he never actually proposed. He *ordered* me to marry him."

Juliet's eyes grew wide. "Why would he do that?"

Oh, dear. That was a slip. The last thing she wanted to tell her innocent younger sister was that he'd ordered her to marry him while they sat naked together in the very bed where they both sat now.

"It's complicated." She waved her hand.

"I have all the time in the world. Since I hope to be courting for the purpose of marriage next year, I would like to know everything you've experienced so far."

That was the one thing she did not want Juliet to say. Heat rose up her body, her heart pounded, her nipples tightened, and her face flushed. She gave her sister a nervous smile.

"What?" Juliet said. Then she covered her mouth with her hand. "Oh, no, you didn't!"

***

"Lord Pomeroy has called, sir." Simon's butler, Tanner, handed Simon his guest's calling card. He looked at it with a sinking feeling in his stomach. He had wondered how long Blackwell would hold off informing Pomeroy what Elise had told him. Well, his lordship wouldn't be coming here this morning to demand something Simon hadn't already attempted. Except it was hard to face the man whose unmarried daughter one had bedded.

"Send him in." Might as well get it over with. Perhaps Pomeroy would have some ideas on how to get Elise to consent to marriage because they were at a standstill right now.

The last couple of weeks, he'd seen her at various events, but always kept his distance. He wasn't quite sure who he was punishing—her for not accepting his proposal and insisting on an affair, or him for wanting to surrender just so he could hold her in his arms again.

No matter how hard he'd tried, there were always times during the events when their eyes met, and the sadness in Elise's eyes had the power to bring him to his knees. Apparently his erstwhile lover was as miserable as he was. Except it was her who had rejected him. He'd wanted to do the right thing, but her stubborn nature had refused his offer.

She had danced a few dances with some of the gentlemen, and he smiled the few times she stumbled during the cotillion. It was killing him to see her with other men, but he knew with her being so against marriage, he had no worries there. She still tried to hide behind potted plants and made numerous trips to the ladies' retiring room, apparently falling back on her original plan.

He'd felt like a bloody huntsman, stalking his prey.

"Good morning, St. George." Pomeroy's booming voice echoed through the room, bringing Simon's thoughts front and center.

Simon stood and shook hands with the man. His lordship did not have a weapon pointed at his chest, and for all intents and purposes he appeared jovial, and merely as one gentleman calling on another.

"Please send in refreshments," Simon said to Tanner.

Still on edge, Simon directed Pomeroy to a grouping of chairs. They settled on two comfortable chairs and Simon leaned back, his legs crossed. They chatted amiably about their health, the weather, and the latest goings-on in parliament. Eventually, Simon knew he had to get to it. "To what do I owe the honor of this visit, sir?"

Pomeroy tapped his fingers on the arm of the chair, his eyes boring into his. "I think you know, young man."

Oh, God. Here it comes. If the man came at him, both fists raised, he would go down with dignity and never strike back. He certainly deserved it for ravishing his daughter. No matter that it had been Elise's idea. Something he would never let her father know. He was the man and experienced, and Elise had been an innocent. No. He was to blame, and would take full responsibility.

Simon ran his fingers through his hair. "Yes, sir. I will not insult your intelligence by pretending I don't know to what you refer. Saying I'm sorry means nothing."

Just then Tanner entered with a tray of coffee, warm rolls, and delicious-looking scented pastries. Both men ignored the food and remained in subdued silence until Tanner left and closed the door.

"What do you plan to do about it?" The soft words were spoken with steel behind them.

"I have already proposed marriage to Lady Elise, my lord. She has refused."

Pomeroy nodded his head with no surprise, which led Simon to believe when Blackwell divulged the information to Pomeroy, he was kind enough to include the part about his offer and Elise's refusal. "And you planned to leave it at that?"

Here was where the sticky part came in. He was staying away from Elise because she still wanted an affair, and he was afraid if he spent enough time with her, he would give in. It would be impossible for him to ignore those plump lips, hold her too close in a waltz and feel her curves, then torture himself with memories of how her warm, smooth flesh felt under his hands. How did one explain that to a gently reared woman's father?

It was simple. One didn't.

"No disrespect intended, sir, but your daughter is a bit on the stubborn side."

Pomeroy let out with a genuine hearty laugh. He shook his head and studied the floor, still grinning. Then, with an abruptness that startled Simon, his expression sobered, and, staring him in the eye, Pomeroy blurted out, "Do you love her?"

Simon felt as though someone had punched him in his middle. All the air left his lungs, and he had the strong urge to jump up and run from the house. Mount his horse and race for his country home, never to return to London again.

Did he love her? No. He could not love her. He

saw what love had done to his father. Yet, the past couple of weeks he'd been almost as miserable as his father had been when Mother had taken off with her lover. Except Simon had no child to ignore and hadn't drunk himself into a coma every night.

His thoughts wandered to recollections of Elise stumbling through the cotillion, then laughing herself silly about it. Furiously whacking her ball so hard that she knocked out one of the guests at the Townsend garden party. He pictured her eyes as they stared into his while they waltzed, and how her arms waved around when she spoke to her friends about subjects and events he'd never before heard uttered from a woman's lips.

As uncomfortable as it made him to think of other things while her father sat nearby, nevertheless, he saw Elise in all her naked splendor, stretched out before him, passion in her eyes as she welcomed him without reservations into her innocent body.

Yes, God help him. He loved her.

Simon cleared his throat. "Yes, sir. I love her."

Again Pomeroy nodded as though Simon had merely confirmed what he'd already known. "Then we need to have a plan."

"Sir, I think you should know she already had a plan."

Pomeroy waved him off. "Oh, I knew about that nonsense almost from the start. Why do you think I brought Blackwell into it?"

"*You* brought Lord Blackwell into it?"

"Of course. I had no way of knowing what your true intentions were, but I knew if Elise thought I was taking the choice away from her, she might try a bit harder to bring you up to scratch."

Simon snorted. "Well, she did that, sir. But, unfortunately, it didn't work."

"Are you telling me the seduction of my innocent daughter was her doing?" Pomeroy's frown and low voice were more frightening than standing blindfolded in front of a firing squad.

Bloody hell. Since the man did not seem to be carrying a weapon, a beating was probably in his near future after all. "No, sir. Not at all, sir. She was completely blameless. I take full responsibility."

"Of course."

Simon ran his finger around the inside of his cravat.

"As you pointed out, Lady Elise is a bit on the stubborn side, much like her mother. Wonderful woman. We had eleven delightful years before she was taken from us." He made the sign of the cross, which confused Simon, since he did not know they were Catholic.

"In any event, you must do something to convince her, since there can be no other outcome for this indiscretion."

"Of course not, sir."

"Good." Pomeroy stood and slapped him on the back, probably with a bit more enthusiasm than necessary. "I leave it in your capable hands, my boy."

Leave what in my capable hands? The man hadn't offered anything in the way of ideas or assistance. "Um, Lord Pomeroy, you certainly know your daughter better than I do. Have you any suggestions?"

He waved his finger into his face. "No coercion, she would not stand for that. Or being ordered about. Too strong-willed. Anything but another seduction. Then I will be forced to call you out, and that gets rather messy." He turned and left the room, mumbling about blood, surgeons, and escape to other countries.

Simon stared after him, no more enlightened than when he'd arrived. So he was to convince Elise to marry him, but could not coerce, order, or seduce her.

I wonder if his lordship considers kidnapping acceptable?

CHAPTER TEN

Despite her fatigue and unsettled stomach, Elise joined her sisters and Papa at the entrance hall for a trip to Lord and Lady Belmont's musicale. They had attended it every year, but Elise had mostly been excused from the torture. This year, however, Papa was adamant that she would attend with them. When he announced the event two evenings ago, he not so subtly reminded her that she was in search of a husband, since Lord Blackwell suddenly, and unexpectedly, withdrew his suit.

When Papa had called her into his study to relate that information to her, he'd asked if she had any idea why the man would do that. Even though she knew her face was redder than the finest rose in Mother's garden, she shook her head and feigned ignorance. By the time she'd escaped his scrutiny, she'd been covered in sweat.

All she wanted to do now was return to her bed and sleep. She pushed to the back of her mind the book she'd read years ago that outlined the early stages of pregnancy as extreme fatigue, stomach upsets, and a propensity for tears and swooning.

She continued to cling to the hope that all the upset in her normal life had disrupted her courses. If the worst had, indeed, happened, she would be forced to tell Simon, and he would again *order* her to the church. Was it so terrible that if she were forced to take a husband, she wanted love and a proper proposal? Especially since she'd finally admitted to herself that she was in love with him. Who wanted a man who felt she was no more than self-flagellation for a wrong committed?

Once they arrived at the Belmont home, which was considerably larger than most London townhomes, Elise took her papa's arm and walked with her sisters into the impressive home. Elaborate candelabras hung from the ceiling in the entrance way, as well as in the spacious double drawing room where the musicale was to be held.

Dozens of people had already arrived. Papa and the girls took seats about halfway back from the platform that had been erected on the south wall. They settled in and conversed with those around them. Elise was having a hard time keeping her yawns in, and her eyes open. Juliet sat on her left side and Papa on her right.

He was looking handsome again this evening, and, now more aware of what happened between men and women, she noticed several of the ladies eyeing him and casting him glances that he chose to ignore. She'd always known her parents had a love match, which is why she and her sisters had always expected ones for themselves.

However, it had only been when she'd been thrust into the role of mother and household manager that she'd discovered how much she enjoyed the feeling of independence and freedom the role had afforded her. It hadn't taken her long to question the wisdom of marrying and being under the thumb of a husband.

She flipped thorough the printed program and was impressed that the well-known opera singer, Nellie Melba, was to perform. Hearing the famous singer would be worth passing up an early evening at home.

Not more than fifteen minutes after they arrived, musicians climbed up onto the platform, tuning instruments while their hostess moved to the front of the crowd, causing conversation to die down and eventually cease.

"I am extremely pleased that you all joined us this evening. Once my lovely and very talented daughters have performed, we have the wonderful Mrs. Nellie Melba to entertain you." Lady Belmont beamed in the direction of her two girls sitting in the front row.

Oh, Lord, so they were to be a captive audience for the very un-talented young women in order to enjoy the lovely performance by the opera singer. She sighed, reconciling herself to a headache before the night's end.

The first notes struck up and one of the Miss Whartons began her warble when a hand landed on Papa's shoulder. Without turning around, he immediately rose from his seat, which was quickly filled by Simon.

Elise drew in a sharp breath as he leaned toward her. "Good evening, Lady Elise." His deep, smooth voice had the desired effect. The oh so familiar scent of soap and mint, along with his own unique essence, drifted over her in waves. Why, oh why did her heart have to beat so rapidly and her lungs have trouble accessing air?

She turned to him and her insides melted. She'd missed him so much. He was incredibly handsome, his swarthy fresh-shaven skin above the starched white cravat, his deep blue eyes eating her up, as she was sure hers were doing to him. His soft smile did her in.

Good grief, she felt tears well up—another symptom—and blinked rapidly to dispel the pending disgrace. She turned away from him, fussing with her skirts as she tried desperately to focus on the singer. His large hand covered hers, stilling the movements. Unable to look at him, instead she stared at their hands, remembering . . .

Slowly, Simon tugged on her gloves, pulling them over her skin, one inch at a time, the silky material sliding over her sensitive flesh. Once her hands were bare, he removed his gloves and intertwined their fingers. Skin-to-skin, flesh-to-flesh, she closed her eyes and felt as raw and exposed as if she were sitting there naked.

His thumb skimmed over the inside of her wrist, stroking, caressing, and drawing small circles on her skin. The area between her legs drew damp, her nipples tightened, and she tried desperately to access air for her lungs. The man had turned her into a wanton. Here she was in a public place and all she could think about was ripping her clothes off and climbing onto his lap. Her nervous giggle escaped.

He leaned in once more, his warm, sweet breath bathing the sensitive skin by her ear. "Are you well, my lady?"

Drat, again tears threatened. She couldn't stay near him, couldn't breathe, couldn't look him in the eye without blurting out her fears and throwing herself into his strong arms. Black dots danced in front of her eyes, threatening a swoon.

"Excuse me." Without looking at anyone, she yanked her hands free and quickly rose, her gloves dropping to the floor. Stumbling along, she passed those next to her, apologizing as she continued on down the line, edging her way past the other guests.

Once free of the room, she rushed down the corridor, as if in pursuit, to the entrance hall and the surprised butler. "Lord Pomeroy's carriage, please."

Not wishing to speak with anyone, she stepped outside and waited on the steps, her arms crossed over her body, hugging herself, and shivering in the dampness, wishing she'd remembered her shawl. Once the carriage drew up, she hurried down the steps, blinded by tears, and instructed the driver to deliver her home and return the carriage for her sisters and Papa.

A footman helped her into the vehicle and stepped back. She settled in and just as the door started to close, the front door of the Belmont's home flew open and Simon stepped out, holding her gloves. His eyes searched the area until they landed on her carriage as it slowly rolled away.

"Elise!" His voice echoed in the night air, mixed with the sound of carriage wheels.

And her sobs.

***

Simon cursed and pounded the doorframe with his fist, then leaned his forearm against the wood and hung his head, her gloves dangling from his hand. What the devil went wrong? He'd planned with Pomeroy to take his seat once the music began so he could spend time with Elise. Try to talk some sense into her. Instead she fled like Cinderella, with him holding her gloves instead of her shoe.

He pushed himself away from the door to return to the drawing room. Then, deciding he had no desire to stay since she'd left, he turned on his heel and asked for his carriage to be brought around.

The ride home went by too fast and, before he knew it, they'd pulled up to his townhouse. He considered going to Elise's home instead, but knew with the rest of the family at the musicale, if he went to her house they would end up making love, and he had promised her father he would not seduce her again.

Instead, he wearily climbed the stairs to his study, poured himself a brandy and sat, sprawled in a chair, staring out the window at the darkness, planning his next move.

Barely after ten o'clock the next morning, Simon looked up from his desk where he perused the financial news from *The London Times*. Tanner entered the room looking agitated. Since Simon had never seen the man in any demeanor except composed, he was curious as to what had the butler so troubled.

"My lord, two young ladies have come to call." He sniffed his disapproval.

Simon's brows rose. "Two young ladies? Here?"

"Yes, my lord. I left them on the front steps since I don't think it is proper for young ladies to be calling on a bachelor."

"For heaven's sake, Tanner, if they are true ladies, leaving them outside the door is even worse." He jumped up from his seat and strode through the study door to the entrance hall, flinging the front door open.

Lady Juliet and Lady Marigold stood on the steps, glancing nervously from side to side. "Oh, bloody hell." He grabbed Lady Juliet by the arm and dragged her through the door. Lady Marigold followed.

Simon shook his head and placed his hands on his hips. "What are you two doing here? Do you realize if anyone saw you it would be instant ruination for the both of you?"

"We had to speak with you, my lord." Lady Juliet stuck her chin out, staring him down. Apparently Elise was not the only stubborn and headstrong Smith daughter. No wonder Pomeroy wanted to see them all married off.

He ran his fingers through his hair. "Well, since you're already here, come into the drawing room. But," he pointed his finger at them, "as soon as you have your say, you will go directly home. How did you get here anyway? I'm surprised your driver would agree to bring you to my house." Simon was always amazed at how more aware of strictures servants were than members of the *ton* sometimes were.

"We hired a hackney."

He groaned. "Oh, Lord. It gets worse." He waved them up the stairs. "Second door on the right." He turned to Tanner. "Have Cook send in tea and biscuits. And tell Spencer to ready my carriage to drive the young ladies home."

Once they were all settled, both girls properly sitting on the edge of a settee, hands in their laps, the picture of decorum, Simon said, "What is so important that you would both risk your reputations by calling at the home of a bachelor?"

"Elise."

Just the one word from Lady Juliet was enough to set his heart beating in double time. Dear God, had something happened to her? She was obviously distressed when she left him last night. "Is she unwell?"

They looked at each other, which had his stomach muscles tightening. "What is it?" Their silence was beginning to terrify him. Perhaps he should have gone to her home last night after all.

Lady Marigold nudged her sister. "Tell him."

"My lord, our sister is suffering from a melancholy. She won't eat, she doesn't sleep well, and she weeps." Lady Juliet blurted out the words. "I am sure you know her well enough to realize that is not her normal behavior."

Before Simon could process that information, Lady Marigold added, "And, we are quite certain her behavior of late has to do with your lordship." The girl ducked her head, obviously not as bold or headstrong as her sisters.

"No doubt." Simon stood and walked to the window, his hands behind his back. "I tried to speak with her last evening, but I'm afraid that didn't go well. I must admit I am at a loss as to what to do next."

"'Tis simple, my lord." Lady Marigold's soft voice had him turning around to see both girls smiling brightly. "We have a plan."

He groaned. Another plan.

***

"I don't want to go to a poetry reading." Elise faced her sisters and father at the breakfast table. "And I certainly do not want to attend with Lord Blackwell."

"I am sorry, my dear, but I am afraid Blackwell obtained these tickets before he withdrew his suit." Papa looked remorseful enough. "He asked me if you would still attend with him, and I thought it would be quite kind of you to agree."

"This is ridiculous. I am sure there are many women in the *ton* who would be thrilled to be invited to a poetry reading with Lord Blackwell." Why in heaven's name would the man want her to accompany him after what she'd told him? In fact, truth be known, she would be a bit embarrassed to face him, anyway, given what she'd confessed the last time she'd seen him.

"My dear, you need to resume your social life. You have been hiding in your bedchamber far too long," Papa said.

Elise huffed. "I have not been hiding! I am simply suffering from some sort of an ague, that is all." She tried, unsuccessfully, to ignore the looks passed among her family members. Why wouldn't they leave her alone? It was obvious her papa had planned for Simon to take his seat at the musicale several days ago.

She still could not believe how she'd fallen apart at being so near to him after weeks of estrangement. If she had not escaped, there was no doubt in her mind that she would have flung herself into his arms and wept out all her agony and fears. She had to stay strong. The last thing she wanted from Simon was pity and a feeling of "duty" toward her.

Papa shook his head. "I am afraid Blackwell will be so disappointed." He picked up his fork and continued to eat.

Now Elise felt guilty as she pushed the eggs around her plate. Blackwell had been quite gracious when she told him she could not marry him. He had even held that secret from her father, as well. The roof would have come down on her head had he revealed to Papa what she and Simon had done. She sighed. "Very well. I will go."

Why ever would her sisters look so happy? Everyone was acting strangely, and she needed to get away. With breakfast over, it was time for her morning ride. She still hoped exercise would bring on her courses. But, alas, with the other symptoms that plagued her, there was little chance of that. Of course, she could go for her usual ride on Pearl and throw herself off. Except she could kill herself, and if she was truly breeding, she did not want to harm her baby.

Her baby.

Tears flooded her eyed again. Her and Simon's baby. "Excuse me." She rose and left the table, her meal half-eaten, and walked out the garden door. She inhaled deeply of the fresh morning air, feeling a bit better.

Lord Blackwell held his hand out as Elise stepped from his carriage. The poetry reading was being held in Hatchard's book store, which was a surprise to Elise because she'd been there earlier in the week and there had been no advertisement for a poetry reading.

They entered the room, and to Elise's further surprise, her friends from her intellectual gatherings were all there. She was happy to see them since they represented normalcy in the crazy world her life had been of late.

They greeted each other, and then she and Blackwell took their seats. He settled her on the aisle seat and took the one next to her. They chatted amiably for about ten minutes, then Miss Henrietta Gordon stepped to the front of the gathering.

"Good evening, everyone. Tonight will be a special treat for our little group. We have only one speaker to read to us, but I think we will all be pleased with his performance."

Elise heard more people enter the room and turned to see her sisters and Papa join the group. Juliet and Marigold took the seats behind her, and Papa leaned against the wall, his arms crossed over his chest.

What in God's creation was going on? Her heart began to pound with suspicion. Was this another of Papa's schemes to get her and Simon together? She moved to stand when Blackwell put his hand on hers. "Stay."

Shocked by his actions, she stared at him wide-eyed when Simon walked to the front of the room and turned to face the group. He had a paper in his hand and looked directly at her. She eased herself back into her seat. Her face flamed, and she thought she would surely faint dead away into Lord Blackwell's lap.

There was conflicting emotions in Simon's eyes. Determination, uncertainty, and something else she was afraid to consider. He cleared his throat and lifted his paper. "Those of you who know me well," he looked directly at her, and all the blood left her face, "are aware that not only do I not like poetry, but I would never write any of my own."

Write poetry? Simon? Oh, good Lord, was he about to embarrass himself and everyone else by reading poetry he wrote? She held her breath.

"So, in view of that, I have resorted to borrowing a poem by George Lyttelton, 1st Baron Lyttelton, who has written words that are in my heart, words I would write if I knew how to do this sort of thing."

He began to read.

When Elise on the plain appears
Awed by a thousand tender fears
I would approach, but dare not move:
Tell me, my heart, if this be love?

Whene'er she speaks, my ravish'd ear
No other voice than hers can hear,
No other wit but hers approve:
Tell me, my heart, if this be love?

Elise sucked in her breath and was sure the sound of her heart thumping would drown out his words.

If she some other youth commend,
Though I was once his fondest friend,
His instant enemy I prove:
Tell me, my heart, if this be love?

When she is absent, I no more
Delight in all that pleased before
The clearest spring, or shadiest grove:
Tell me, my heart, if this be love?

Simon moved from in front of the group, walked toward her, and spoke from memory the last lines with which she was very familiar.

When fond of power, of beauty vain,
Her nets she spread for every swain,
I strove to hate, but vainly strove:
Tell me, my heart, if this be love?

He lowered the paper and looked at her. "Is this love? Because either I am madly in love with you, Lady Elise, or I need to consult with a physician in the morning to discuss my ills."

When the tightness in her throat kept her from answering, she merely nodded. With a relieved expression on his face, he dropped to one knee and took her hand. "Lady Elise Smith, will you please make me the happiest of men and marry me? I love you and don't want to go even one more day without knowing you will be mine forever."

"You substituted my name for *Delia* in the poem." Her fingers wiped tears from the corner of her eyes and her voice shook.

"Oh, my love. Only you would find fault in what I had hoped was the best proposal ever offered." His grin softened his words.

With tears streaming down her face, she said, "Yes, my Lord St. George, I will marry you."

He stood and swept her into his arms to the rousing cheers of her intellectual friends, who she was surprised to learn, had a romantic bent to them. Once Simon released her, she realized the one person in the room cheering the loudest was Papa.

CHAPTER ELEVEN

Simon breathed a sigh of relief as he looked down at his betrothed. If this crazy plan of her sisters hadn't worked, he was at a complete loss as to what to do next. He'd been determined to marry her for quite some time, but when Lady Juliet hinted that Elise might be with child, he'd been tempted to simply walk up to her house, throw her over his shoulder, and head for Gretna Green. Which, he assumed, would be with her father's blessing.

But probably not Elise's, and she was the one with whom he would have to spend the rest of his life. Amicably.

They were soon separated, with her friends and family wishing them well. His father-in-law-to-be slapped him on the back. "Well done, young man. I didn't think you had it in you. All that poetry drivel."

"I certainly don't have it in me to write it myself. And after spending hours poring over one awful poem after another, I was only too happy to use this one. And replace *Dalia* with *Elise*." He chuckled. "She would notice that."

"Yes, well, she's all yours now, St. George." He seemed very happy, and to emphasize it, gave him another hardy slap on the back.

One of the ladies in the group had brought a

cake that they all shared. And Lord Pomeroy's footman, who appeared from nowhere, offer glasses of champagne.

After about an hour of conversation and good cheer, he noticed Elise was looking a bit wan. They needed time to speak in private and the trip home from the bookstore would be a good time to get a few things settled. Hopefully she would agree to a quick wedding since he already had the special license in his pocket. If nothing else, he was optimistic.

He took her hand as she spoke with Lord Westin. "My dear, I think perhaps an early night might be welcomed?"

Her grateful look had all the protective instincts in him rearing up. If she was, indeed, increasing, he would move them to the country as soon as they married. Fresh air, long walks, and healthy food were the best things for an expectant mother. It amazed him at how his heart sang over the possibility of having a child of his own. Something he swore for years he would never have. A wife whom he loved, and a child he would never abandon in any fashion.

"Yes, I believe I would like to leave soon."

They said their goodbyes, Lord Pomeroy still glowing with happiness, and Lady Juliet and Lady Marigold, as well. Their plan had worked, Pomeroy had one less daughter's bills to deal with, and Elise's sisters were now free to pursue husbands.

He helped her into his carriage and directed the driver to Elise's townhouse. Despite the need to discuss important matters, the ride remained silent with Elise resting her head on Simon's shoulder.

Simon kissed her on her head. "Perhaps we can discuss our plans in the morning?"

Elise looked up, her eyes wide. "I thought perhaps you could stay for a while, and we could—talk."

The hesitation in her question had his cock cheering as loud as Pomeroy had. He had to be sure what she meant, however. He placed his lips against her temple. "What do you have in mind, sweetheart?"

She drew circles on his chest. "Well, you refused to consider an affair, and since I have agreed to marry you . . ."

Yes!

He would not be breaking his word to her father since he promised not to seduce her into saying she would marry him. She'd already consented, so . . .

In one swift movement, he had her on his lap, and his lips covered hers. He groaned with satisfaction. Her taste, her scent, all those soft curves, combined to make him ache so hard, he doubted he could walk. He considered tapping on the ceiling and having the driver continue on, but that would be deuced uncomfortable.

Once the vehicle came to a stop, he hopped out and turned to assist her. He quelled the urge to sweep her into his arms and race up the stairs. There was Mason, the staid butler at the front door to consider. With as much control as he could master, Simon walked sedately by her side into the entrance hall. "Good evening, my lord, my lady." Mason gave them a stiff bow. "Will you require tea?"

"No, thank you, Mason. Lord St. George and I will not require refreshments. We will be in the drawing room for a while."

They ascended the steps to the first floor, then continued on past the drawing room to the second floor where the bedchambers were. They walked softly so as not to alert Mason that they were not in the drawing room.

Elise giggled.

Simon took a candle from the box at the top of the stairs and lit it with one of the sconces along the wall, and they entered her bedroom. He immediately touched the flame to the candle branch in her room. The little bit of illumination was just enough for him to see Elise somewhat clearly.

She stood in the middle of the room, a shy smile on her face. Slowly, she undid the ribbon on her bonnet and dropped it to the floor. Her gloves went next, followed by her half boots.

When she raised her skirts to remove her silk stockings he moved with swiftness to stop her. “Leave your stockings on.”

Her brows rose, and then she dipped her head in acquiescence. She turned. “Unfasten my gown?”

With shaky, fumbling fingers, he unfastened the gown and allowed it to slip to the floor. Her petticoat, stays, and chemise were next, joining the pile of discarded clothing at her feet. Once she was naked, except for her stockings, he wrapped his arms around her from behind, settling his hands on her more than slightly rounded belly.

He closed his eyes and sucked in a breath, kissing her neck. Leisurely, he moved his hands up to cup her larger than he remembered breasts. Her nipples peaked and begged for his attention. Her pregnancy was obvious to him. Even though they’d only made love once before, his hands had memorized every dip and curve on her body.

Not wanting to have the conversation about that

now, he continued to caress and fondle her breasts and stiffened nipples. Her head fell to the side as he nibbled on her ear. "God, have I missed you. You have no idea how many nights I wanted to crawl through that window over there and come to your bed, to take you."

She turned. "Why didn't you?"

"I didn't want you for one night, darling, I wanted you forever. Had we gone your way with an affair, I would not have been happy, and I believe that eventually you would not have been either."

She undid his cravat. "I hate to admit it—since I am always right—but in this instance I believe you are correct." She shook her head and looked into his eyes. "I want you for always, too, my love."

He groaned and crushed her to him, taking her mouth with such passion and force he almost frightened himself. No longer able to breath, he released her mouth and within seconds he had all his clothing off, joining Elise's garments in a heap. His hands lifted her so her swollen breasts were even with his mouth. "Wrap your legs around me," he mumbled against her breast, taking the silky mound into his mouth, his tongue circling her nipple.

Tucking her legs around him, she fisted her hands in his hair as he walked them to the bed where they tumbled onto the counterpane, arms and legs tangling together. Their hands and mouths were everywhere, reaching, teasing, sucking, kissing, and licking, until they were both breathless and more than ready to come together.

Simon looked down at her as he slowly entered her warmth. "I love you, Elise. Forever and always. You complete me, make me whole, and give my life meaning. I promise you I will be the best husband ever." His eyes closed, and, with a groan, he shoved all the way in. "You will never regret marrying me, I promise."

Elise smoothed her hand over the hair covering his forehead. "I love you, too. So much so that I felt broken when we were apart. You make me whole, also." She gave him a soft smile. A smile he wanted to see for the rest of his life. "Now please love me."

"As you wish, my love. As you wish." He kissed her gently as he began the dance of lovers until they were both panting and groaning each other's names.

***

Three weeks later

Despite Simon haranguing her about marrying sooner since he had a special license, Elise held firm on having a proper wedding. Even though everyone in her family knew she was increasing, she refused to bow to what everyone else wanted. If she were going to go against all she believed in for the past few years, and actually take—gasp—a husband, she would do it the right way.

Simon had been ecstatic about being a father, which, she had to admit, did take her by surprise. He'd told her one night as they sat in the drawing room about his mother abandoning him and his father drinking himself to death. She felt such sorrow for the young boy who had been left to raise himself into manhood with no more guidance than a guardian, who immediately placed him into school and forgot about him.

She'd thought it funny, then no longer amusing, when Simon refused to come to her bed after the night they'd become betrothed. Of course, he was correct that it was disrespectful to her father to climb into her window each night, but she could have gone to his home.

That he had forbidden with raised eyebrows and a lecture on the reputation of his child's mother.

But eventually the day arrived, and Elise stood before her mirror looking at herself as a bride. Her pale blue dress, shot through with silver, made her feel like a fairy princess. All the feelings she'd had as a young girl, when she still believed there would be a Prince Charming in her future washed over her. Yes, she did look like a fairy princess, and her knight in shining armor awaited her downstairs.

"Oh, Elise, you look absolutely lovely!" Juliet sailed into her room with Marigold right behind her. They were both dressed in pale rose gowns, with matching flowers in their hair. Juliet's gown was a bit lower in the neckline and had cap sleeves, while Marigold's was more demure, as fitting a younger lady.

Elise studied Juliet in her mirror, almost as if seeing her for the first time in weeks with the wedding preparations taking up so much of her time. Juliet had lost weight, her cheekbones more prominent, and her face was quite pale. But the telling sign of a disturbance was the sadness in her eyes. Juliet's eyes always sparkled with life and humor. "Juliet, are you unwell?"

"No, I am fine, why do you ask?"

"No reason." Elise continued to watch her.

Her sister's smile faded as quickly as it had come. Something was troubling Juliet, and as swept up as Elise had been with her own happiness, she had overlooked a problem that she was sure Juliet was suffering with. When she'd really looked at her sister last had been at the arranged poetry reading when Juliet had hugged her and expressed happiness at her betrothal.

This was not the same girl.

She moved toward her sister and placed her hand on her forehead. "Are you sure, sweeting? You are not looking well."

Juliet snapped her head away. "I am fine. I just told you." Glancing at the look of surprise on her two sisters' faces, she rearranged her features into something more pleasant. "Truly, I am fine. It is your wedding day, Elise. We must focus on you, and not on nonexistent problems."

Whatever the nonexistent problem was, Juliet was obviously not willing to share it. Rather than spoil her wedding day, Elise pushed it to the back of her mind and put her arms around her sisters' waists. "Shall we go downstairs and see about this marriage business?"

Both girls grinned at her, and they left the room.

Simon stood at the altar, chatting with the vicar and Lord Amsley, who was to be his witness. All three men were tall, but Simon stood out with his broad shoulders and classic aristocratic features. He was outfitted in all black except for a white waistcoat and cravat. He looked magnificent, and she once again marveled that this wonderful man loved her.

Elise walked toward him on her father's arm, a bit more nervous than she would have thought. Once her father kissed her on the cheek and handed her over to Simon's care, all her anxiety fell away like a shattered piece of fine china. She looked up at her soon-to-be husband and grinned.

He grinned back.

The exchange of vows took place in a small church outside of London, with only a few close friends and family members attending the ceremony. The Pomeroy townhouse would hold about eighty guests for the wedding breakfast to follow.

Although it was not a common practice, Simon gave Elise a quick kiss once the vicar pronounced them man and wife. They turned to face their family and friends, and made their way down the aisle to sign the wedding register with their witnesses and the vicar.

"This is a proper kiss for my new wife." Simon leaned into her as the carriage carrying them away from the church entered the London traffic. He cupped her face in his hands and nibbled and kissed her lips until she was ready to skip the breakfast.

Despite her desire to speed through the breakfast, Elise enjoyed the repast very much. Cook had hired extra help and the spread of different types of eggs, rolls, three different fish, bacon, roasted vegetables, and a beautifully decorated cake was varied enough to please any guest.

Simon spooned an extra helping of eggs onto her plate. "You are eating for two, my dear." His voice was lowered so only she heard him, for which she was grateful.

"If you keep feeding me this way, my love, I will soon appear as though I'm eating for three or four."

He raised his eyebrows. "Perhaps you are."

She stopped, her fork halfway to her mouth.

"Oh, dear. I hope not."

An orchestra started up, Papa walked up to her, and extended his arm. "May I have a dance with my beautiful daughter before her husband takes her away from me?"

"Oh, Papa." Her voice quivered and tears sprang to her eyes. "I will always be your daughter, you know."

They moved to the dance floor. "Of course you will. And I will have a word with St. George before you leave to make sure he knows I will be watching. He is to treat you like fine porcelain."

She drew back. "Me? Fine porcelain?"

He considered for a moment, then said, "Hmm, well, perhaps sturdy kitchen crockery." He turned her and they waltzed away, their laughter ringing in the air.

The End

Did you like this story? Please consider leaving a review on either Goodreads or the place where you bought it. Long or short, your review will help other readers discover new authors and make purchasing decisions!

Want to read more Regency romance from Callie Hutton? Turn the page for an excerpt from *Marrying the Wrong Earl*, Book 2 in the Lords and Ladies in Love series.

MARRYING THE WRONG EARL

Chapter One

London, England, April 1820

Lady Arabella Danvers stared in horror as the Earl of Pembroke groaned and slid his vast body off the settee, landing with a thump onto one knee. He took her hand in his fleshy, sweaty one. "My lady—"

She sucked in a breath. "No, please, my lord. Do rise. Sit alongside me." She patted the settee, frantic to keep him from proposing. She'd known for some time what his intentions were but had hoped her lack of interest would have dissuaded him. Of course, she'd been well trained in how to word a refusal-of-marriage offer, but each time she'd had to do it, she'd suffered for days afterward seeing the pain of rejection in the gentleman's eyes.

"I must say this, Lady Arabella. I have admired you for some time now. You must know of my interest—"

"Perhaps I should send for more tea…" She attempted to tug her hand loose from his grip, to no avail. Her mother had left the room several minutes ago, leaving her not properly chaperoned, so apparently, Pembroke's fumbling attempt at a proposal was not a surprise to Mother.

"I hold you in a great deal of esteem." He continued on as if she hadn't spoken. "I would at this time like to ask you—"

"My lady?" Arabella breathed a sigh of relief as the butler, Tavers, entered the drawing room. "Lady Elizabeth and Miss Caroline Davis have come to call."

She smiled brightly at Lord Pembroke. "Perhaps you should rise, my lord."

He glowered at the butler then gave Arabella a wan smile. "Yes, yes, of course. I will continue this another time." He awkwardly shifted his girth to stand but instead fell halfway, practically landing on her.

"Lady Arabella, how wonderful to see you." Lady Elizabeth and her cousin, Miss Caroline Davis, glided into the room. Pembroke rearranged himself, red faced and puffing, attempting to regain his dignity. Arabella hopped up to greet her guests. The three kissed the air next to each other's cheeks, exclaiming over gowns and bonnets. No one seemed to notice Lord Pembroke, who gave a soft cough.

"Oh dear, my lord, I did not see you there." Lady Elizabeth gave him a slight curtsy, as did Miss Caroline, who murmured, "My lord."

"Good afternoon, ladies." He turned to Arabella. "I will leave you now to visit with your friends. May I have the pleasure of escorting you on a drive tomorrow afternoon?"

Lady Elizabeth and Miss Caroline both turned to Arabella with raised eyebrows.

"Yes, indeed. Lady Arabella would love a ride tomorrow afternoon, wouldn't you, dear?" Arabella's missing mother, Lady Melrose, hurried into the room, all sunshine and happiness.

"Actually, Mother, I had planned to…" She halted, unable to think fast enough.

Mother jumped right in. "Nonsense, a ride in the park would be just the thing. You spend far too much time doing whatever it is you normally do in the afternoons." She took Lord Pembroke's arm and walked him out of the room, her voice fading as she chatted away.

"Lord Pembroke?" Lady Elizabeth adjusted her skirts as she settled on a chair across from the settee where Arabella sat. "I had no idea."

"There is no idea. I know the man intends to propose, but I will not be accepting." Arabella filled teacups for herself and her two visitors. "Although I am not foolish enough to want love in a marriage, I would at least prefer to like the man I'll spend the rest of my life with." She shuddered as she took a sip of her tea. "And I can assure you, that will not be Lord Pembroke."

Miss Caroline took a small biscuit from a tray on the table in front of them. "It sounds as though your mother has other ideas."

"Yes, I know. I do wish she would stop pushing me to marry. Due to Papa's declining health, and then his death, I started late, so I've only had one Season. Is it so terrible for me to not take the first man who offers marriage?"

"Pembroke is the third man you have turned down, young lady." Lady Melrose swept into the drawing room, a frown marring her still-lovely complexion. A frown Arabella had noticed was, of late, a perpetual expression for her once-carefree mother.

Since Arabella was an only child, the family estate had passed into the hands of a distant relative who was currently conducting business in India. They had been told by their solicitor the new Earl of Melrose was expected to return to England and take up residency in the fall.

Unfortunately, Arabella's late father had enjoyed a predilection for whiskey and faro, and a total lack of interest in the preservation of his estate. Mother had impressed upon Arabella several times that once her dowry was paid, there would be no funds left for her support, so unless her daughter took her in, she would have nowhere to live.

Via their solicitor, the new earl had offered to allow Lady Melrose to continue living at the estate, but her mother had turned up her nose at that offer. She would live with her newly married daughter, she'd sniffed.

"I've hardly turned down three ideal offers, Mother. Lord Pembroke never got the words out, and Mr. Featherington and Baron Smythe are both old enough to be my grandfather."

"Which is to your advantage, miss. They are both wealthy men and will die soon."

At Arabella's indrawn breath, her mother waved her hand. "No need for hysterics, young lady. It is a fact that both men were looking for a wife in order to have an heir before they cocked up their toes."

And I do not wish to be someone's broodmare.

If she said that out loud her mother would most definitely swoon, and a half hour would pass trying to restore her sensibilities. Instead, Arabella waved at the teapot. "Would you care for some tea, Mother?"

Lady Elizabeth and Miss Caroline had pretended they hadn't heard the exchange by softly mumbling to each other. But Arabella had no doubt they took in every word and would soon use it as fodder for their next morning call. Honestly, why couldn't Mother be a bit more circumspect?

"No tea, thank you, daughter. I am off to the milliner's. I will see you at dinner before we depart for the Ashbourne ball."

Arabella groaned inwardly at the reminder. At present, one of Arabella's animal patients was in dire need of supervision while it recovered from its injuries. The last time she had left one of the downstairs maids in charge of a patient, the poor thing had died.

Mother thought her concern for animals, and her desire to nurture them back to health, a nasty hobby. On the other hand, Arabella saw it as a way of keeping her brain from melting with all the talk of ribbons, gowns, gossip, and other nonsense most of the ton ladies lived for.

She'd already heard whispers at various events about her passion for animals and how unseemly it was for a young lady to delve into such goings-on. She sighed. Another reason she so disliked attending these functions.

Later that afternoon, Arabella entered the spare bedchamber where she kept the various animals under her care. The scant sunlight coming though the west window cast a soft glow over three dogs, one bird, and two cats. All had been injured in some way. She had been rescuing and treating animals since she was a young girl. Over Mother's objections, Arabella continued to not only bring home injured animals, but accept those poor creatures that appeared at the back door of their townhouse. Despite the whisperings at social events, word of her healing skills had spread throughout London, and those unable to care for their injured pets brought them to her.

She could not remember a time when she did not love caring for animals. As a young girl, more comfortable with the family's groom than other girls of her class, she'd spent time learning about horses and their care. That knowledge had driven her to various books on veterinary practices, and then eventually to helping other injured animals.

"Well, look at you, Miss Aphrodite. You appear well today." She addressed the large white long-haired cat which ran her pink tongue over her fur. The animal continued her ministrations, ignoring Arabella. Something she did on a regular basis. The gash on the left side of her body was slowly healing. Arabella had sewn her up, and did her best to keep the cat from licking the wound.

Arabella would bring the cat to the elderly Lady Oswald, who had agreed to take Miss Aphrodite when Arabella had mentioned her to the ladies at her morning calls. Arabella placed the basket on the floor and carefully lifted the cat and placed her inside. "I know you will just love your new home. Lady Oswald is quite anxious to have your company."

Since it was a pleasant day, Arabella and her maid, Sophia, elected to walk through the park to reach Lady Oswald's house. The air was unseasonably warm, and the soft breeze tickled the hair that had escaped her bonnet, blowing the wisps into her eyes.

The blanket over the top of the basket where Miss Aphrodite rested began to shift. "I believe our passenger has awakened from her nap."

Lifting the blanket, Arabella stared down at the animal, who stared right back at her. Before she could even say a word, the cat jumped from the basket and raced away.

"Miss Aphrodite, come back!" Arabella handed the basket to Sophia then picked up her skirts and, abandoning all dignity, dashed after the cat. "Come back," she yelled, ignoring the people around her who turned to gawk in her direction.

The cat tore over the ground, apparently chasing a small rodent. Arabella placed her hand on her bonnet, which threatened to sail from her head. The cat continued on, and Arabella was beginning to get a stitch in her side when a young gentleman headed toward her from the other direction. Right in Miss Aphrodite's path. "My lord, can you please catch my cat?"

Apparently deep in thought as he enjoyed a stroll, the man looked up just as the rodent ran up his leg. Miss Aphrodite hurled herself at his chest, the weight of her body knocking him backward into a tree. Waving his hands to avoid the mouse and the cat, he slammed into the trunk, slid down, and landed in a puddle of muddy water. His hat flew off, and Miss Aphrodite jumped from his shoulder onto the tree, scaling the branches, disappearing from sight.

***

Nash, the Earl of Clarendon, stared stupidly at the woman who raced up to him, holding her side and panting. "I'm so sorry, my lord. Are you well?"

"Lady Arabella?" With his legs stretched out, he

shook his head, trying to clear it, and stared up at her. He remembered her from a few social events they'd attended together. If his memory was correct, she was a friend of his sister, Eugenia, Marchioness of Devon.

"Yes. Oh, my goodness, Lord Clarendon. I am so very sorry." Her face was flushed, her bonnet askew, her eyes—for lack of a better word—wild. That look, however, did not detract from the girl's visage. Lady Arabella was, indeed, a very attractive young lady. Not that this was the time to dwell on such a thing.

He placed his hand on the soft, muddy ground and jumped up. The back of his breeches clung to him in such a way that he knew they were mud filled. As was his glove, he noticed with chagrin. "What happened?"

"My cat." She continued to pant and barely got the words out.

"Your cat?"

"Yes. She got out of my basket." She pointed behind her to where a woman, obviously a maid, hurried up, carrying a basket with a blanket draped over it. Lady Arabella looked behind him, up at the branches of the tree. "Oh dear. She's climbed up, and now she can't come down."

Just as she uttered the words, a loud howl came from above. The devil take it, was the animal now going to drop on his head?

Lady Arabella glanced frantically from the top of the tree to him. "My lord, can I ask a favor of you?"

Still trying to process everything that had just happened, he looked at her for a minute before answering. "A favor?"

"Yes, please. Can you climb the tree and rescue

my cat?" She chewed her lower lip, which would have appealed to him if he wasn't standing in wet, muddy breeches, with an animal yowling over his head.

"Climb the tree?" Surely the woman was daft. This was Hyde Park, for heaven's sake, not his country estate where he'd done such things as a lad. "I am sorry, my lady, but I fear I am not dressed for tree climbing. Animals are most adept at rescuing themselves."

She waved at the animal howling above his head. "What sort of a gentleman are you? You would walk off and leave that poor animal in distress?" Her voice rose on the last few words.

Nash glanced around at the two couples who strolled nearby, who were watching the exchange with a bit too much interest and humor. The last thing he wanted was to draw more attention to himself.

"Please?" Apparently, she felt a change of tactics would work better. Her irresistible hazel eyes filled with tears, and her plump lower lip quivered. Bloody, bloody, hell. The one thing he could not countenance was a woman's tears. He ran his hand down his face before he remembered his glove was muddy.

She winced.

"I just smeared mud all over my face, did I not?"

She nodded and continued to chew her lip. At least she had the good sense not to laugh, as he was sure she was wont to do. The cat continued to screech, and to his horror, a crowd was gathering. "Very well." He stripped off the muddy gloves, then his coat. The sooner he got the blasted animal out of the tree and back into its basket, the sooner he could go home, have a bath, and down a very large glass of brandy.

"Oh, thank you so much." She stood, wringing her hands. "Yes, well. Let's have at it." He grabbed a low-lying branch above his head and swung himself up. He balanced on the branch and reached, but was not high enough to grab the irritating cat.

"Miss Aphrodite, come down, please. Let this nice gentleman help you."

Nash looked down, his eyes wide. "Miss Aphrodite?"

"Yes. That's her name."

Miss Aphrodite.

"If you call her by her name she might warm up to you and come down," she shouted up at him.

He was already making a spectacle of himself in the tree, his arse covered in mud, and dried, caked dirt on his face. He would damn well not call the animal by that ridiculous moniker. "Come here, kitty."

That sounded no better. The cat wailed and looked down at him. He grabbed another branch and moved higher. Reaching out, he almost had her when she hissed and leaped right at him, her nails clinging to his waistcoat. "Ouch!"

He grabbed the animal by its back fur just as a loud sneeze erupted from his nose. Nash wrapped his arm around the branch next to him as he sneezed several more times.

"Oh, my lord. Are you allergic to cats?"

He looked down at Lady Arabella. "I've never been this close to one before, so apparently, I am, my lady." He began his descent, trying to hang on to the hissing, scratching cat. More sneezes. "I will drop the animal, if you can catch it."

"Oh, no, my lord. She will just run off again."

Bloody hell. The best thing that could happen to

any of them was to have the blasted cat run off. As far away from him as possible. He continued to hang on to the feline until he jumped to the ground. He heard the sound of fabric tearing as his feet landed. Nash closed his eyes and groaned when he realized the back of his breeches had just split.

With a scowl, he turned the cat over to Lady Arabella, who purred and talked nonsense to the devil-feline. She tucked the creature into the basket and covered it with the cloth once more.

"I suggest you remove that animal before it runs off again." He took out a handkerchief and attempted to brush some of the dried dirt from his face.

"How can I possibly thank you, my lord?" Lady Arabella's face shone with happiness as she tucked the blanket snugly around the basket. The animal did not move, seemingly worn out from its adventure.

"You can thank me by never allowing that—thing—out of the house again." He sneezed once more and wiped his nose. He retrieved his coat from the grass and shrugged into it, hoping it covered enough of his breeches to allow him a dignified retreat from the park. "Now, I will bid you good day, Lady Arabella." He bowed as if he wasn't covered in mud, with a tear in his breeches, and his face dirty. Turning on his heel, he strode out of the park and toward his townhouse.

***

Later that evening, Nash descended the stairs to the Ashbourne ballroom to join his sister, Eugenia, and her husband, Lord Devon. He squashed the urge to turn tail and run when he noticed Lady Arabella standing next to Eugenia, chatting away. Just watching her, he felt a sneeze coming on. She certainly looked a lot better than she had the last time he'd seen her. Of course, he imagined he looked more restored, as well.

Earlier, his valet, Andrews, had sniffed his disapproval at the condition in which Nash had returned home. With raised eyebrows, but no comment—none was necessary—he had helped Nash out of his clothes and, holding them by his fingertips, marched across the room to drop them into a bundle on the floor. "A bath, my lord?"

"Yes. But a large glass of brandy first."

"Indeed."

Pushing the scene from his mind, he stepped up to the group. "Good evening, Lady Arabella, Eugenia, Devon."

"Oh, Lord Clarendon." Arabella extended her hand. "Thank you once again for rescuing my cat. Well, actually, she really wasn't my cat—"

"Excuse me?" Had he suffered indignities and angered his valet for naught? "Not your cat?"

"Yes. You see, I was delivering the cat to Lady Oswald when Miss Aphrodite escaped."

"Then it was Lady Oswald's cat?"

"Well, yes, sort of."

He knew he should just drop the subject, but Eugenia and Devon eyed him with curiosity, so he felt the—foolish—need to ask, "Would you care to explain, my lady?"

"I rescued Miss Aphrodite from an alley on Oxford Street after a very bad cat fight. I sewed up her injuries and took care of her until she healed. Lady Oswald expressed a desire to own a cat, so I offered her Miss Aphrodite. I was delivering her when she ran off this afternoon."

"You rescued Lady Arabella's cat, Nash? How very sweet." Eugenia smiled at him in such a way he felt ridiculous. No one had ever called him sweet before. Nor would anyone ever again, if he had anything to say about it.

He'd gotten disgustingly muddy, torn his breeches, suffered from sneezing fits—all to rescue a cat that probably belonged in the wild anyway. Anxious to turn the conversation, he extended his hand to Eugenia. "May I have the privilege of this dance, sister?" The orchestra was just starting up a cotillion, and he wished to be gone from Lady Arabella's company before he hurled insults at her and her animal.

"No. This baby is giving me a bit of stomach upset." She placed her hand on her tummy. "I'd heard morning time was the problem, and although I have some difficulties with my breakfast, lately evening seems just as troublesome. We will be leaving shortly."

"After a good night's rest, we are off to the country early tomorrow morning." A sly grin crossed Devon's face, and he bent down to whisper in Eugenia's ear. She drew in a sharp breath, and a deep shade of red rose to her cheeks.

Nash groaned, not wanting to know what his brother-in-law had said. "All right, you two. Devon, remember, Eugenia is my baby sister. I do not wish to know what it was you whispered to her, but please discontinue before I feel the need to ask you to step outside."

A wide grin split his brother-in-law's face. "She's my wife!"

"And my sister!"

"Enough!" Eugenia laughed and placed her hand on Nash's chest. "All is fine. I promise." She fanned herself and cast a sideways glance at her husband, who studied her with a look which Nash preferred not to be aware.

Deciding he had had enough of their infatuation with each other, he bowed and kissed Eugenia's cheek. "I shall leave the two of you to toddle on home. 'Tis difficult for me to stand here while smothered with all this love floating around. Have a safe journey tomorrow."

Lady Arabella looked back and forth between Lord Clarendon and Lady Devon. "I believe felicitations are in order?"

"Yes." Eugenia smiled. "We are expecting an heir in several months." She turned to Nash. "Since we are leaving, I am sure Lady Arabella would be delighted to join you in this dance, brother."

He groaned inwardly. Hell and damnation. He'd been trying to get away from the chit. Only disaster could loom on the horizon when this woman was involved. But, drawing on his manners, he bowed. "Lady Arabella, would you honor me with this dance?"

Purchase Information

http://calliehutton.com/book/marrying-the-wrong-earl/

ABOUT THE AUTHOR

Callie Hutton, the *USA Today* bestselling author of *The Elusive Wife,* writes both Western Historical and Regency romance, with "historic elements and sensory details" (*The Romance Reviews*). She also pens an occasional contemporary or two. Callie lives in Oklahoma with several rescue dogs and her top cheerleader husband of many years. Her family also includes her daughter, son, daughter-in-law and twin grandsons affectionately known as "The Twinadoes."

Callie loves to hear from readers. Contact her directly at calliehutton11@gmail.com or find her online at www.calliehutton.com. Sign up for her newsletter to receive information on new releases, appearances, contests and exclusive subscriber content. Visit her on Facebook, Twitter and Goodreads.

Callie Hutton has written more than 25 books. For a complete listing, go to www.calliehutton.com/books

Praise for books by Callie Hutton

A Wife by Christmas

"A *Wife by Christmas* is the reason why we read romance...the perfect story for any season." --The Romance Reviews Top Pick

The Elusive Wife

"I loved this book and you will too. Jason is a hottie

& Oliva is the kind of woman we'd all want as a friend. Read it!" --Cocktails and Books

"In my experience I've had a few hits but more misses with historical romance so I was really pleasantly surprised to be hooked from the start by obviously good writing." --Book Chick City

"The historic elements and sensory details of each scene make the story come to life, and certainly helps immerse the reader in the world that Olivia and Jason share." --The Romance Reviews

"You will not want to miss *The Elusive Wife*." --My Book Addiction

"...it was a well written plot and the characters were likeable." --Night Owl Reviews

A Run for Love

"An exciting, heart-warming Western love story!" --*NY Times* bestselling author Georgina Gentry

"I loved this book!!! I read the BEST historical romance last night...It's called *A Run For Love.: --NY Times* bestselling author Sharon Sala

"This is my first Callie Hutton story, but it certainly won't be my last." --The Romance Reviews

A Prescription for Love

"There was love, romance, angst, some darkness,

laughter, hope and despair." --RomCon

"I laughed out loud at some of the dialogue and situations. I think you will enjoy this story by Callie Hutton." --Night Owl Reviews

An Angel in the Mail

"…a warm fuzzy sensuous read. I didn't put it down until I was done." --Sizzling Hot Reviews

Visit www.calliehutton.com for more information.

Made in the USA
Middletown, DE
20 April 2019